THE CASE OF THE
Beautiful Beggar

Erle Stanley Gardner

THE CASE OF THE

Beautiful Beggar

WALTER J. BLACK, INC., ROSLYN, N. Y.

THE CASE OF THE
Beautiful Beggar

Chapter ONE

Della Street, Perry Mason's confidential secretary, regarded the lawyer with pleading eyes.

"*Please* see her, Chief."

Mason frowned. "I have this ten-thirty appointment, Della, and before I see this man I want to— Oh, well, I don't want to ruin *your* day. What's it all about?"

"She's just arrived in Los Angeles from the Orient. She came by way of Honolulu. She has a letter from her uncle telling her to get in touch with you immediately upon her arrival here and before she goes home."

"And she didn't send a wire asking for an appointment?" Mason asked.

"She isn't that kind," Della said. "She's about twenty-two, naïve, demure, quiet-spoken and very much disturbed."

"She was told to see me immediately on arrival?"

"That's right. Her uncle, Horace Shelby, wrote her a letter and —"

"What's in the letter?"

"I don't know. She said that her uncle had told her not to show it to any living mortal except Perry Mason."

Mason sighed. "Show her in. I'll hit the high spots, get rid of her and—"

Like a streak Della Street went through the door to the outer office before he had finished the sentence.

Mason grinned and rose as Della ushered in a beautiful young woman.

"This is Daphne Shelby," she said, and then, smiling brightly at Daphne, "and this is Mr. Mason."

Daphne shyly mumbled a greeting, opened her purse, took out a letter, said, "Thank you very much for seeing me, Mr. Mason. I guess I should have sent a wireless but I was too upset. . . . I'll try and be as brief as possible."

Della passed the letter and envelope across to Mason.

The lawyer held the envelope in his hands for a moment while he sized up Daphne.

"Won't you sit down?" he asked.

She seated herself somewhat tentatively in the straight-backed chair across from his desk, rather than in the comfortable overstuffed leather chair usually selected by clients.

Mason regarded her thoughtfully. "How old are you?" he asked.

"Twenty-two."

"You wanted to see me about your uncle?"

"Yes. Horace Shelby."

"How old is he?"

"Seventy-five."

"He's your uncle?" Mason asked.

"Yes," she said, noticing Mason's uplifted eyebrows. "I'm the daughter of Robert Shelby who was eighteen years younger than Horace."

"Is your father living?" Mason asked.

"My father and mother were killed in an automobile accident when I was one year old. Uncle Horace sent for me and raised me."

"He's married?" Mason asked.

"No, he's a widower, but he had a wonderful woman keeping house for him. She was like a mother to me."

"Is she still with him?"

"She died two years ago. . . . Please, Mr. Mason, I feel that after you read that letter, you'll see the urgency of all this."

Mason unfolded the letter addressed to Daphne Shelby care of the steamship at Honolulu and marked *Urgent*.

The letter was in pen and ink and in the cramped, wavering handwriting of a person whose reflexes are somewhat impaired by age.

The letter began,

Daphne dear,

Don't come home until you have done what I am asking. Don't let anyone know you have heard from me. I won't be able to meet the boat. Take a cab and go as fast as possible to the office of Perry Mason, the attorney. Get Perry Mason to go to the bank with you; cash the enclosed check and have Perry Mason take charge of the money for you so that it can't possibly be found by anyone.

After you have done this, come home and try to keep your temper. Be prepared for a shock.

Tell Perry Mason to prepare a will leaving everything to you. I want a short will and I want it prepared just as fast as he can do it. Have Mr. Mason come to the house when the will is ready for my signature. Tell him to have the necessary witnesses with him. At the very first opportunity he's to hand me the will. I'll sign it and give it back to him to keep. No one except Mason and the witnesses must know he has a will ready for my signature, or that it has been executed. The greatest secrecy is necessary.

Please remember, Daphne, that no matter what happens I love you very much indeed.

Your Uncle Horace.

Mason read the letter, frowning thoughtfully. "Sounds like an emergency. Do you have any idea what it is?"

"The letter is all I know. It was sent to Honolulu. I had been in Hong Kong for a three-month vacation. They thought I needed a rest."

"Who is the 'they'?" Mason asked.

"The brother, Borden, and his friend."

"Borden Shelby?" Mason asked.

"No, his name is Finchley. He's a half brother. He and his wife came to visit Uncle Horace. He brought his friend, Ralph Exeter, and since Aunt Elinor was there it was suggested—"

"Aunt Elinor?" Mason asked.

"That's Borden's wife. She said she'd take charge of things. They agreed that I was rundown and needed a good long rest; that I was to go on an ocean voyage and forget about everyone except myself."

"And you've been away several weeks?"

"Nearly three months."

Mason extended his hand casually. "There was a check in the letter?" he asked.

She passed over a slip of paper. "Here it is," she said.

Mason looked at the check, suddenly straightened in the chair, frowned, looked at the check again and said, "This check is for *one hundred and twenty-five thousand dollars!*"

"I know," she said. "I couldn't understand it at all."

Mason pursed his lips. "Quite evidently there's something bothering your uncle." The lawyer looked at his watch. "All right," he said, "let's go to the bank and cash this check. Are you known there?"

"Oh, yes, I've done my uncle's banking business."

"And he has a balance sufficient to honor this check in his commercial checking account?"

"That's right. There was around a hundred and forty-five thousand dollars in it when I left. I keep his books and make out his checks you know."

"But he signs them?" Mason asked.

"Oh yes."

Mason gave Della Street a troubled glance. "That ten-thirty appointment," he said, "explain that I've been unavoidably detained for just a few minutes. . . . Now, what do you want done with this money, Daphne, you can't go around carrying a sum like that."

"No, no, the letter says you are to take charge of it and fix it in such a way that I can have it but nobody can find it."

Mason frowned. "I don't think I care to undertake something of that sort, but I can certainly arrange to keep the money for you until we can find out what this is all about.

"You have some cash with you?" he asked as they started for the door.

"Actually I don't. Uncle Horace saw that I had traveler's checks when I started on the trip. But everything was a lot more expensive than we had expected. I cashed my last traveler's check in Honolulu. I had just enough money for taxi fare here. I'll have to take taxi fare home out of the money we get on this check.

"You see," she added apologetically, "I hadn't expected anything like this, and the cost of the taxi here was a lot more than—Well, I'm broke."

"I see," Mason said. And then as they started down the corridor to the elevator added, "Your Uncle Horace is wealthy?"

"Quite wealthy," she said. "That is, I consider him so. He has some real estate holdings and stocks and bonds, and he keeps a large amount of liquid cash."

"I can see that he does," Mason said. "Why?"

"He likes to have cash on hand that he can use whenever he wants to for quick investments without bothering to sell stocks or bonds."

They went down in the elevator, walked two blocks to the bank, and Mason said to Daphne, "You know one of these gentlemen at the teller's window?"

"Oh, yes," she said, "I know several of them. There's Mr. Jones over there. There's a short line in front of his window."

She took her place in the line. Mason stood beside her.

The line thinned out at the window, and Daphne endorsed the check, then pushed it through the wicket.

"Why, hello, Daphne," the teller said, reaching for the check. "A deposit?"

"No, I'm cashing this check," she said.

The teller opened a drawer. "All right, how do you want it? You —" He looked at the check, paused in stiff arrested motion, said, "Excuse me for a moment, please."

He left the window, and a few minutes later was back with the cashier.

The cashier glanced at Daphne, then at Perry Mason.

"Why, hello, Mr. Mason," he said.

Mason acknowledged the greeting.

"Is he with you?" the cashier asked Daphne.

She nodded.

The cashier handed back the check. "I'm sorry, Daphne," he said, "but there isn't any money to cover this check."

"No money?" she asked. "Why, I'm sure there is. When I left there was—"

"The account has been cleaned out by a Court order," the cashier said. "It's been transferred to a conservator—I think you'd better see your uncle. Mr. Mason can explain to you what has happened."

"I'm not sure I can," Mason said. "What's the exact status of the account?"

"A court order appointing a conservator. The conservator asked for the balance in the account and wrote a check for that exact amount, transferring funds to an account in the name of Borden Finchley as conservator."

"When did all this happen?" Mason asked.

"Day before yesterday."

"I think I see," Mason said.

The cashier's eyes were sympathetic as he handed the check back to Daphne. "I'm sorry," he said, and then added, "but that's a rather unusual check."

"I know it is," she said. "That's the way Uncle Horace wanted it."

"Well, you'd better have a talk with him, and have a talk with this Borden Finchley. Do you know him?"

"Oh, yes," she said, "he's my uncle too—that is, he's a half brother to Uncle Horace. He's staying there with Uncle Horace."

The cashier flashed a sharp glance at Mason, then turned back to Daphne. "You've been away?" he asked.

"Yes, I went on a vacation nearly three months ago."

"Apparently a good deal has happened while you've been gone," the cashier said, and then glanced at the line that was forming behind Daphne. "Mr. Mason will take care of you, I'm sure."

He gave a reassuring smile and turned away.

Mason took Daphne's elbow. "I think you'd better give me that check, Daphne," he said, "and perhaps you'd better let me keep the letter for you. Now, I have an appointment which I simply can't break. The person is waiting for me up in my office right now, but I think you'd better take a cab and go right out to the house and, if possible, talk with your Uncle Horace. If you can't talk with him, get in touch with me and—"

"But why shouldn't I be able to talk with him?" she asked.

"I don't know," Mason said. "He may have had a stroke or something. You know, a person at that age is getting to a point where those things do happen. I feel certain that there's been a very drastic change in the situation while you were gone, and if for any reason you can't see your uncle, I want you to come right back to my office. You can telephone first and let my secretary, Miss Street, know that you're coming."

Her eyes were dark with alarm. "You think Uncle Horace has—?"

"I don't know," Mason said. "Your Uncle Horace was all right when he wrote that letter, but evidently something has happened. Perhaps he is not getting along well with his half brother."

"Well," she said, "I can understand that. He didn't want them to come and see him in the first place."

"All right," Mason said, "here's twenty dollars for cab fare and expenses. Run along now, get a cab. I'm going back to the office. You give Miss Street a ring. You be sure to let us know what the situation is out there."

The lawyer gave her shoulder a reassuring pat, held up his hand for a cab which was waiting, put Daphne in it, then strode down the street toward his office building.

Chapter TWO

It was just before Mason was leaving for lunch that Della Street said, "She's back, Chief."

"Who is?" Mason asked.

"Daphne Shelby."

"I'll see her," Mason said.

Della nodded and brought Daphne into the office.

"What is it, Daphne? Bad news?" Mason asked.

Her eyes showed that she had been crying. She seemed numb with shock.

"They've done something terrible, Mr. Mason."

"Who has?"

"Borden Finchley, Ralph Exeter and Elinor."

"And what have they done?"

"They've put Uncle Horace away."

With that, she burst out crying.

"Now, take it easy," Mason said. "Keep yourself in hand. Let's find out about this. What do you mean, they put him away?"

"They had him declared incompetent or insane, or something, and they've taken over the house and they've locked up my room and told me that I have until tomorrow night to take all my things out. And they won't tell me what's happened."

"All right," Mason said grimly, "sit down. Let's get this thing straight."

Mason picked up the telephone. "Tell Paul Drake to come in, if you will, Gertie. I have a case for him."

Mason said, "Now, just try to relax for a minute, Daphne. Paul Drake is a private detective and a good one. He has his offices on this floor and he'll be in here within a minute or two.

"In the meantime, I want you to fill me in with a little background."

"What do you want me to tell you?"

"You've been in the Orient for three months?"

"Well, in the Orient, and on shipboard. I took a long cruise. I went to Honolulu, to Japan, to Hong Kong, then to Manila and then back."

"You had letters from your uncle while you were gone?"

"Oh, yes."

"What kind of letters?"

"Nice cheerful letters."

"And then when you got to Honolulu you received this letter?"

"Yes. If I hadn't been in such a hurry to get ashore, I would have had it when the boat docked, and then I could have telephoned or taken a plane or done something. But I had made some friends in Honolulu on the trip over. They were waiting for me and I hurried off the ship as soon as we were cleared to land. I didn't get back until just before the ship sailed.

"So I stood on deck saying goodbye to friends before I went down to my stateroom. The letter was there, waiting for me.

"By the time I had read the letter, the ship was well out past Diamond Head.

"Somehow, the letter itself didn't mean so much to me. I thought that Uncle Horace was a little despondent and he wanted me to have some money that— Well, frankly, Mr. Mason, I thought it was some kind of a tax deal. I thought perhaps he was leaving me money in his will, but wanted me to have some money that wouldn't be subject to inheritance tax."

Mason shook his head, said, "It would have been a transfer in contemplation of death. He didn't send you that check for that purpose —the question is, why *did* he send it?"

"I don't know."

"His letters were cheerful?"

"Well, yes, but come to think of it, there was a little something strained in his letters as though he— Well, now that you mention it, I begin to think of certain things. The letters were sort of stereotyped and—perhaps he wanted me to keep on having a good time and not bother me with anything until I got back."

"Now, when you went out there this morning," Mason said, "what did . . ."

The lawyer broke off as Paul Drake's code knock sounded on the door.

Mason nodded to Della Street, who opened the door.

Paul Drake, tall, loose-jointed, deceptively mild of manner, gave a comprehensive grin by way of greeting.

Mason said, "Paul, this is Daphne Shelby. Sit down while I find out just what has happened. After I get this information from Daphne, we'll make plans, but right now getting this information is too important to justify any interruption."   ·

Mason turned back to Daphne. "Tell me what happened when you went to the house," he said.

"Well, of course," she said, "I was worried and I was in a hurry to see Uncle Horace, so I didn't wait for anything but just used my latchkey and ran right in and yelled, 'Whooooo-hoooo! Here I am!'

"No one answered. I looked right away into the room Uncle has and it was vacant, both his study and his bedroom. So then I ran up to my room and my room was locked."

"You had a key to it?" Mason asked.

"Heavens no. When I left there was a key on the inside of the bedroom door, but I never kept it locked."

"But it was locked just now?" Mason asked.

"That's right. So I went looking for Uncle Borden or Ralph Exeter or Aunt Elinor or somebody."

"And who did you see?"

"Aunt Elinor."

"And what happened?"

"Aunt Elinor smiled and said, 'Oh, hello, Daphne. Did you have a good trip?' And I said, 'Yes. What happened? Where's Uncle Horace?' And she said, 'Your Uncle Horace had to be taken away. He's in a home where he'll be given the best of care. And we suppose you, of course, will want to move out just as soon as you can get your things together.'

"So then she smiled at me, a cold, frosty smile, and said, 'We've locked up your bedroom so that your things will be safe. We'd like to have you out by tomorrow night because Borden is figuring on renting the house furnished. It will bring in a very tidy sum.' "

"Go on," Mason said.

"Well, I just looked at her in consternation and said, 'Why, this is my home. It's been my home ever since I was a baby. I'm certainly not going to move out. I'm going to see Uncle Horace and find out what this is all about.'

"Then suddenly Aunt Elinor got hard. I'd never seen her get hard before. She was just like cold granite. She said, 'Indeed, you're *not* going to stay here, young lady! You've sponged off your uncle long enough.' And I said. 'What do you mean, I've sponged off him? I've been taking care of him and getting all rundown doing it. Why you, yourself, told me that I had been working too hard and I needed to take a three months' vacation.' "

"What did she say to that?" Mason asked.

"She said that she had found out a lot of things about me since I had left and that her husband had been appointed conservator of Horace Shelby's property and he certainly intended to conserve the property and keep it from being wasted and dissipated, or given to shrewd and designing persons. She said that she had evidence I was intending to play Uncle Horace for a good thing and get all of his money and that I had been too greedy even to wait for his death, but had been milking him right along and that his housekeeper, prior to her death, had been milking him and I had been standing in with her and helping her do it."

"Then what?"

"By that time I was in tears. I guess I made a horrible scene. I couldn't stand up to her and I couldn't listen to those awful things she was saying. I turned and ran out of the house and she called after me that I had until tomorrow night to move my things out of the house. Otherwise, she would have to move them herself."

"And then?"

"I'm afraid I was hysterical. I—All I could think of was getting to you just as fast as I could, because . . . because something horrible has happened.

"I know now that they are just schemers, that they moved in on Uncle Horace, took advantage of his generosity and good nature and got me out of the place on the pretext that I needed a rest and a vacation and then, just as soon as I was gone, they ganged up on Uncle Horace in such a way that they irritated him past all endurance. And Uncle Horace, of course, knowing that I needed a rest and a vacation, thought too much of me to tell me anything about it in his letters, but tried to act as though nothing was happening."

Mason frowned thoughtfully and said, "The fact that your uncle sent you that check indicates that he thought he had a little more time than he did—or perhaps he felt you could take a plane back. In any event, they moved in more rapidly than he had anticipated and evidently had a court hearing."

Mason turned to Della Street and said, "Della, get hold of the clerk of the court, find out what department the Shelby hearing was in day before yesterday, what judge granted the order, and the status of the case at the present time."

He turned to face Paul Drake. "Paul, I want you to find out where Horace Shelby is now. They probably moved him by ambulance. They have some doctor who may or may not be in on the conspiracy, and they've probably been using dope of some kind."

Mason said to Daphne, "Have either of your uncles or your aunt had any experience with medicine, or any medical education?"

"Why, yes," she said. "Aunt Elinor was a trained nurse."

"I see," Mason said grimly. "There are some drugs that can calm an elderly person when he gets excited and there are some that throw him entirely off his mental balance. I'm afraid you have been the victim of a rather deep-seated conspiracy. . . . How much is your Uncle Horace worth? Do you have any idea?"

She frowned thoughtfully and said, "Well, at least a million dollars. Probably more, what with his real estate, his stocks and bonds."

Mason was thoughtful for a moment, then said, "Paul, I want you to find out something else. You have a pipeline into banking circles. They won't give you confidential information, but they will give you all the information that isn't confidential, everything that's a matter of record.

"Now I want you to get to this bank and find out just what happened to the account of Horace Shelby."

Della, who had been on the phone, said to Mason, "The order appointing Borden Finchley as conservator for the estate of Horace Shelby was made by Judge Ballinger day before yesterday. Borden Finchley qualified with a bond and immediately proceeded to take charge."

"All right," Mason said, looking at his watch, "I happen to know that Judge Ballinger's secretary stays in his chambers until twelve-thirty. Ring the secretary and see if I can make an appointment with Judge Ballinger for one-thirty, if possible. In any event, I want to see him before he goes on the bench this afternoon. Tell him it's very important."

Della Street nodded, got busy on the telephone, and after a few moments said to Perry Mason, "He isn't expected in until just before court, but if you'll be there at one-forty-five, you can at least see him for a few minutes before he goes on the bench. The judge had a luncheon engagement today and may not be back until just before court."

"All right," Mason said, "I'll go to see him."

He turned to look at Daphne Shelby's forlorn face.

"Where's your baggage?" he asked.

"Right in the taxicab," she said. "I never did get it unloaded from the cab because I have no place to put it. . . . I know all this is horribly expensive. I'm living on borrowed money and I guess I don't have a cent to my name."

"That's all right," Mason said. "We'll see that you're taken care of temporarily."

She said, "I . . . I suppose I can get a job somewhere, but this is such a shock to me."

Mason turned to Della Street. "Della, go down and help Miss Shelby get a room in one of the downtown hotels. Go to the cash drawer and get a couple of hundred dollars so that you'll have plenty of money and leave her with enough to cover expenses."

"Oh, Mr. Mason," Daphne said, "I can't do that. I don't want to be a . . . a beggar."

Mason smiled at her and said, "Quit crying, Daphne. If all beggars were as beautiful as you are, it would be a wonderful world. . . . But you're not a beggar, you're a client and I'm a lawyer."

"But I can't pay you anything, and the way things look now, I don't know if I ever can. Tell me, if Uncle Horace left a will in my favor and they have found it and just burned it up, what could be done?"

Mason's face was stern. "Probably nothing," he said, "unless we can prove that such a will was in existence and they had burned it. Do you know if he made such a will?"

"He told me that he was going to."

"His letter," Mason said, "indicates that he hadn't done it. I may as well prepare you for the worst, Daphne. You've been the victim of a very clever conspiracy. Also it's a conspiracy that is as old as the hills. A wealthy man has relatives. Some of the relatives are close to him; some of them are not. The relatives who aren't close to him come to visit, get themselves established in the house, get rid of the relative who is close to the old man, then take advantage of the absence to claim the old man is mentally weak and subject to being exploited by shrewd and designing persons. They have themselves appointed conservators, tear up any will they may find and so put themselves in a position of sharing the estate."

"But can't . . . can't he make a new will?"

"Not after he's been declared incompetent," Mason said. "That's the beauty of the scheme."

"But how can they get a person declared incompetent when he's really in full possession of his faculties?"

"That," Mason said, "is the diabolically clever part of it. You take any man who is past a certain age, who is accustomed to love, devotion and loyalty, then surround him with people who are willing to commit perjury; who constantly irritate him and perhaps are willing to use drugs, and the first thing you know you have a man who seems to be incompetent.

"But what I'm afraid of is that he may have walked into a trap."

"What do you mean, a trap?" she asked.

"That letter to you," Mason said.

"Why, what about it? He just wanted me to be taken care of no matter what happened."

"Of course he did," Mason said, "but if they walk into court and say, 'Here is a man who gives his niece a check for a hundred and twenty-five thousand dollars and tells her to put the money where it can't be found—well, such a person needs a conservator of his estate.'"

Daphne's eyes grew large and round. "Do you mean that they used this letter—"

"I think perhaps they did," Mason said. "I don't know, but I think perhaps they did."

"However, you go with Della Street. I'll fill Paul Drake in on some of the details. He'll start work, and before two o'clock I'll have seen Judge Ballinger. By that time, we'll know a lot more about this."

"And what about my things out at the house?"

"You leave your things right there for the moment," Mason said, "unless there is something that you need."

"But they told me I had only until tomorrow night."

"By tomorrow night," Mason said, "You may be in the house and they may be out."

"But Mr. Mason, I . . . I don't know how I'm ever going to pay you."

"We'll work that out," Mason said. "Right at the moment, remember that I'm an officer of the court, a high priest at the temple of justice. You're a naïve individual who has been the victim of a very great injustice. As a matter of principle I'm to try to rectify it.

"Now, you go with Della."

Mason nodded to Della Street and said, "Be sure she has some lunch, Della, and you get some, too."

Chapter THREE

Judge Ballinger came bustling into his chambers at twelve minutes of two.

"Hello, Perry," he said. "Come in. I'm sorry I'm cutting things so fine as far as time is concerned, but I had a rather important luncheon appointment."

Mason followed the judge to his chambers and watched while the judge put on his robe.

"Got to go on the bench at two o'clock," the judge explained. "I can hold it off maybe a minute or two. What's the problem?"

Mason said, "I think perhaps I'm going to appear before you in your court on a contested matter and I don't want to jeopardize your position or mine by discussing it, but I do want to get some history and, if possible, find out the reasoning back of an order you made in the case."

"What's the case?"

"The matter of the Horace Shelby conservator."

"Why, I handled that just a couple of days ago," Judge Ballinger said.

"I know you did."

Judge Ballinger looked at him shrewdly. "You think there's anything wrong with the case?"

Mason said, "Let's not either of us discuss anything except the history, but I would appreciate your thinking."

"I'll discuss any guardianship matter any time," Judge Ballinger said. "In those cases the Court wants all the information it can get.

"Mind you, I don't want you to tell me anything you feel should come before me by way of evidence in a contested matter, but I'm certainly willing to tell you how I felt.

"Horace Shelby is an old man, and he's confused, there's no question about that, and he was incoherent. He was excited, emotional and apparently he'd made a check for a hundred and twenty-five thousand dollars to some young woman who had been living in the house with him.

"Now, when you get a combination like that, you figure that something needs to be done. I appointed the conservator on a temporary basis with the statement that the Court would review it at any time any additional facts came up."

The judge stopped talking and looked at Mason. "You feel that you have some other facts?"

"I think it's possible," Mason said.

"All right," Judge Ballinger said. The order is subject to review with additional facts. Tomorrow morning at ten o'clock too early for you to present your facts?"

"I think not," Mason said.

"Tomorrow morning at ten o'clock— No, wait a minute, I've got another case on at ten. We'll convene court early. Make it nine-thirty. Tomorrow morning at nine-thirty we'll have another hearing.

"I'm not going to ask to have Horace Shelby brought into court, because I think the court hearing upset him. I'll take a look at any additional facts that are presented and then if I want to amend, suspend, modify the order I made, I'll do it. That suit you?"

"Fine," Mason said.

"Prepare notice to the other side with an order shortening time and all the rest of it," Judge Ballinger said. "I'm two minutes late now."

He shook hands with Mason and walked from chambers into the courtroom.

Mason left Judge Ballinger's chambers, hurried back to his office and entered through the reception room.

He nodded to Gertie, the receptionist, and asked, "Is Della back?"

"Back about twenty minutes ago," she said.

Mason went in to the inner office.

"How did you do, Della?" he asked.

"Everything's okay," she said. "The poor child could hardly eat a bite. . . . Isn't that the darnedest thing you ever heard of?"

"It happens more frequently than we like to contemplate," Mason said.

"How did you do with Judge Ballinger?"

Mason grinned and said, "Make an order shortening time and an order for an additional hearing tomorrow morning at nine-thirty. See that it gets served on opposing counsel. By the way, who is the attorney in the case?"

"Denton, Middlesex and Melrose," she said. "The junior partner, Darwin Melrose, was the one who appeared in court."

"That's a good firm," Mason said. "They wouldn't any of them be mixed up with anything that was off-color—not if they knew it, and they'd be pretty apt to look into it before they went into a case.

"Have you heard anything from Paul Drake?"

"Not yet. He's trying to get something from the bank."

"Well, get those orders out," Mason said, "and arrange to get them served. Also, ring up Daphne and tell her that we're going to court tomorrow morning at nine-thirty: that I want her here at the office at nine o'clock; that she can go to court with me. . . You'd better look in on her this evening, Della, and keep her from getting too upset."

Della nodded and asked, "How was Judge Ballinger?"

"Well," Mason said, grinning, "the judge doesn't want to discuss anything which may come before him where there's a contest, but the judge wasn't born yesterday and he knows as well as anyone the manner in which relatives can act like the proverbial camel in the tent—first put in a head and then gradually get the whole body in and squeeze the occupant of the tent out into the cold."

"He didn't say so, did he?" Della asked smiling.

"No, he didn't *say* so," Mason said, "but the judicial mind was working rather rapidly, I thought."

"This should be quite a hearing tomorrow morning," she said.

"Could be."

Drake's code knock sounded on the door.

"There's Paul Drake now," she said. "I'll go out and get those orders ready and get them served."

She opened the door and said, "Come on in, Paul, I've got a rush job to do. The boss just came in. He has a rehearing for tomorrow morning at nine-thirty."

"Not a rehearing," Mason said, "a hearing to take additional evidence."

"Well I've got some evidence for you," Drake said.

"What is it?"

"Stanley Paxton, vice-president of the bank," Drake said, "is pretty much worked up about this. He wants to do anything he can."

"Will he testify?"

"Sure, he will. If he knows there's a hearing tomorrow morning, he'll be there."

"Go on," Mason said, "tell me about Paxton." "Paxton is the vice-president of the bank who keeps an eye on all the active accounts, particularly the large ones."

"How well does he know Horace Shelby?"

"He knows him mostly through his business transactions. Most of the personal contact that he had was with Daphne."

"What does he think of Daphne?"

"Thinks she's one of the nicest young women he's seen in a long time. He thinks she has a good business head on her shoulders, and he thinks Horace Shelby is being railroaded into a position where he can't make a will that will stand up in court, and these relatives, the Finchley's are moving in on the estate just for the purpose of seeing what they can get out of it."

"And just what will Paxton testify to?"

"That every time he saw Horace Shelby, the old man seemed to know exactly what he was doing; that he has talked with him about investments on the telephone several times; the conversations have been just what one would expect in dealing with a normally sharp businessman and that Horace Shelby has the greatest love and affection for Daphne; that he relies on her for virtually everything and that she has been loyal to his interests all the way through.

"He'll also testify that he never heard of Borden Finchley or Elinor Finchley or their friend, Ralph Exeter, until Daphne went on her trip; that while Daphne was on her trip, Borden Finchley was offensively curious. He was trying to pump Paxton to find out the extent of Shelby's holdings, his net worth and all the rest of it. He tells me that Bordon Finchley gives him the impression of being a chiseler, a sharpshooter and that if anyone has selfish and ulterior motives, it's this same Borden Finchley."

"Well, of course, he can't testify to that," Mason said.

"Not in so many words," Drake said, "but Paxton is a pretty shrewd individual. You get him on the stand and start asking him questions about Horace Shelby and he'll find some way of letting the judge know how he feels about Borden Finchley."

"What about Ralph Exeter?" Mason asked.

"Exeter seems to be a kind of a barnacle on the ship," Drake said. "No one knows his exact connection with Finchley. Of course, he doesn't have any with Shelby."

"You're sure of that?"

"Reasonably. Remember that I've been working at pretty high speed and haven't had a chance to check everything I want, but apparently Finchley is indebted to Exeter for a rather large sum of money and Exeter was pressing for collection, so Finchley brought him along to visit his rich brother so Exeter could see for himself that Finchley was going to run into a big sum of money one of these days."

Mason's eyebrows lowered slightly as he became thoughtful. "That," he said, "would make quite a picture. And, of course, Exeter would have found that Horace Shelby intended to leave everything to Daphne and . . ." A slow grin spread over Mason's face.

"Paul," he said, "Exeter is the weak link in the chain. I want to find out everything you can about the indebtedness of Borden Finchley to Ralph Exeter. Get everything you can about Exeter's background. When Finchley gets on the stand, I won't cross-examine him about Shelby, I'll cross-examine him about Exeter. . . . How did you get this information, Paul?"

"There's a housekeeper who comes six hours a day."

"Who does the cooking?"

"Elinor Finchley is doing the cooking now. Before the Finchleys came Daphne did the cooking. Shelby's wants are rather simple, and Daphne knew exactly what he wanted and how to prepare it. She was doing a whale of a job, but she was working herself to death.

"Then after the Finchleys and Exeter moved in, why Daphne was simply floored. They had this housekeeper in and had a catering service send in many of the meals. That's how they were able to get Daphne to take this long ocean voyage. She was doing the best she could to be a hostess as well as taking care of her uncle's personal needs and cooking his food for him the way he wanted it."

Mason grinned and said, "Paul, I'm not making any promises but I think tomorrow morning at nine-thirty we're going to have a court hearing that will be very, very, very interesting.

"However, in the meantime, you'll have to get a line on Ralph Exeter. I want his background. I want the basis of his relationship to Borden Finchley; and, if Borden Finchley owes him money, I want to find out about it."

"He owes him money all right," Drake said. "The housekeeper heard Exeter telling Finchley that he didn't intend to wait forever and that he wasn't going to sit on the sidelines and wait for somebody to die; that he wasn't built that way; that he wanted to get his money and get a turnover on it.

"Then they saw the housekeeper was standing by the doorway and they changed the subject abruptly."

Mason nodded. "Get Exeter's background," he said, "and I don't care how many men you have to put on the job."

Chapter FOUR

Promptly at nine-thirty, Judge Ballinger ascended the bench and said, "This is the matter of the conservator for the estate of Horace Shelby. The Court stated at the time of making the order that the Court might require additional evidence from time to time and was keeping the matter open.

"The Court now wants to hear additional evidence. Mr. Mason, you have something to present?"

"I do," Mason said.

"Do you wish to present a witness or affidavits?"

"I have an affidavit," Mason said, "from Daphne Shelby, the niece of Horace Shelby, stating that up to three months ago, when she was persuaded to take a long ocean voyage, leaving Horace Shelby in the house where Borden Finchley, his wife and Ralph Exeter were visiting, Horace Shelby was in good mental health and in possession of all of his faculties.

"I have an affidavit from Stanley Paxton of the Investors National Bank, where Horace Shelby has kept his account for many years, stating that Shelby is, in his opinion, thoroughly competent; that Shelby has shown good business judgment in handling all of his affairs; that his properties have grown in value over the years; that he has made shrewd business investments; that Daphne Shelby has always had his best interests at heart and has made a very efficient manager.

"This affidavit further states that from the moment Daphne Shelby was persuaded to take a trip Borden Finchley started nosing around, trying to get information about Shelby's personal financial affairs, trying to wheedle information out of the bank on the pretext that Shelby was ill.

"The affidavit states that Paxton called Shelby on the phone and that Shelby's manner was perfectly normal and his business judgment very sound.

"On the strength of the showing I am about to make, Your Honor, I suggest that the conservatorship be vacated; or, if there is any necessity for a conservator, that Daphne Shelby, who has now returned from her trip, is much better qualified to act as conservator than is Borden Finchley.

"And as a part of my showing, I desire to call Borden Finchley as a witness."

Judge Ballinger frowned down at Finchley. "Come forward and be sworn, Mr. Finchley. You've already been sworn in this matter, but I think I'll have you sworn again just so there can be no misunderstanding."

Borden Finchley, a stocky, rather thick-necked individual in his late fifties, held up his hand, took the oath, then occupied the witness stand and glowered at Perry Mason from rather small, cold, blue eyes.

"Now, your name is Borden Finchley. You're a half brother of Horace Shelby and you were the moving spirit in asking for the appointment of a conservator?" Mason asked.

"That's right," Finchley said.

"You are visiting at Shelby's house?"

"Yes."

"How long have you been visiting there?"

"About six months."

"In other words, you were there for about three months before Daphne Shelby left on her vacation?"

"Yes."

"Who is in the house at the present time, Mr. Finchley?"

"My wife, Elinor, and Ralph Exeter."

"Ralph Exeter?" Mason said, putting just the right element of apparent surprise in his voice. "And is Ralph Exeter a relative of Horace Shelby?"

"He is not."

"A close friend, perhaps?"

"Not of Horace Shelby. He is a close friend of mine. He came to the Pacific Coast with us. In fact, we were driving in his car."

"And you moved right in with Horace Shelby?"

"We stopped to visit Horace and when we saw that he was weakening mentally, we stayed long enough to size up the situation."

"And Ralph Exeter helped you size up the situation?"

"He was with us and we were in his car. We couldn't very well ask him to move on. We imposed upon his good nature by holding him here while the situation was coming to a head."

"And when you say 'coming to head,' you mean that it was getting to a point where you could ease Daphne Shelby out of the picture and put yourself in charge of the Shelby finances?"

"I mean nothing of the sort. I mean that Ralph Exeter was good enough to forego his own personal plans in order to stay with me until the situation was clarified."

"And what do you mean by 'until the situation was clarified'?"

"Until my brother wouldn't be taken advantage of by some young woman who was flaunting her charms, wheedling him for money and finally using her powers of persuasion to get him to turn over to her a hundred and twenty-five thousand dollars in the form of a check on his account, and asking her to go to an attorney to see that the money was handled in such a way that it couldn't be traced."

"I see," Mason said. "You knew about that letter?"

"I knew about it."

"And how did you find out about it?"

"I saw the letter before it was mailed."

"And where did you see it?"

"On my brother's desk."

"You thought the letter was addressed to you?"

"No, I knew it was not addressed to me."

"Did you know to whom it was addressed?"

"I most certainly did."

"And yet you read it?" Mason asked, his voice showing a degree of incredulity that made it appear that the reading of a letter was a heinous crime.

"I read it!" Finchley snapped. "I read it. I called in my wife and had her read it, and I saw the check for a hundred and twenty-five thousand dollars which was to go in the letter, and right then and there I made up my mind that I was going to put a stop to having my brother's estate exploited by a total stranger."

"A total stranger?" Mason asked. "Are you referring to his niece, Daphne Shelby?"

"I am referring to Daphne Raymond, who has been going by the name of Daphne Shelby and who has represented herself to the bank and to my brother's business associates as being his niece. Actually, she is the daughter of his housekeeper and is no blood relation to Horace Shelby."

Mason, veteran courtroom lawyer that he was, managed to keep his face from showing any element of surprise, but simply smiled and said, "You have, I believe, heard your half brother, Horace Shelby, repeatedly refer to Daphne as his niece?"

"I have," Finchley said grimly, "and every time I heard it I knew it was another indication of the fact that Horace's mind was weakening and that the blandishments and wheedlings of this young woman had had their effect."

"But he *is* my uncle," Daphne exclaimed. "He is—"

Judge Ballinger tapped his pencil. "You will be given ample opportunity to state your side of the case, young woman. Just please refrain from making any statements."

Judge Ballinger turned toward the witness. "You have made certain statements, Mr. Finchley. I presume you are in a position to prove them?"

"Certainly, Your Honor," Finchley said. "I didn't care to bring the matter up because I didn't want to blacken the young woman's name, but of course if she insists, we will have to get the facts before the Court."

"What are the facts?" Judge Ballinger asked.

"Marie Raymond was a rather attractive woman who had an unfortunate love affair in Detroit. She came to Los Angeles looking for employment and was penniless, without friends, and had had but little experience and no training in any form of work. She therefore had no alternative but to take up housework. She advertised for a job as housekeeper and it happened that Horace Shelby saw that ad in the paper.

"He arranged an interview. The interview was satisfactory and Marie Raymond went to work for him.

"At that time Marie Raymond rather suspected that she might be pregnant but didn't know for sure. Later on, when she found out that she was pregnant, she confided in Horace Shelby.

"Shelby, at that time, was generous enough to suggest that she go ahead and have the child and continue her employment.

"Later on, when Horace Shelby's younger brother and wife were killed in an automobile accident, Horace Shelby suggested to Marie Raymond that they let the young Daphne think that she was the daughter of the deceased brother and his wife. In that way, Daphne would be given a name and her illegitimacy would not be known to her schoolmates.

"This was done."

"You can prove all of this?" Judge Ballinger asked.

"Certainly, I can prove it. I have letters written by Horace Shelby to my wife and me, letters in which he tells the whole story."

"How did Daphne get her passport?" Judge Ballinger asked.

"On the affidavit of Horace Shelby," Borden Finchley said. "The courthouse at the county seat of the eastern state where the brother and sister had resided had burned, and the birth certificates in the courthouse were consumed in the fire.

"I may state that Horace, while he never remarried after his wife died, had always been very susceptible to feminine charms—that is, to wheedling and importunities. We have no reason to believe that there were any relations between Shelby and Marie Raymond other than that she persuaded him to give her daughter a name and that the daughter used the opportunity to insinuate herself into the affections of Horace Shelby. There is no question but that he regards her with deep affection and there is no question in my mind but that this young woman, being fully aware of the situation, deliberately took advantage of it."

"Where is Marie Raymond now?" Judge Ballinger asked.

"She died a little over two years ago. It was at that time my wife and I decided to look into the situation because we felt that Horace was being imposed upon."

"So you came out here with the deliberate intent of looking into the situation?" Judge Ballinger asked.

"Yes," Borden Finchley said. "Horace is an old man. We didn't intend to have him imposed upon."

"And you wanted to protect *your* interests?" Mason asked.

Before Finchley could answer the question, Darwin Melrose got to his feet.

"If the Court please," he said, "we have been patient in this matter because we felt that, if possible, we would like to keep from bringing out the matters which relate to the illegitimacy of this young woman; but in view of the circumstances which have now been disclosed, we respectfully submit that there is nothing before the Court; that Daphne Raymond, sometimes known as Daphne Shelby, is a complete stranger to the controversy; that Perry Mason, as her attorney, has no status before the Court and is, therefore, not entitled to question the Court's decision or ask questions of the witnesses."

"Well, now just a minute," Judge Ballinger said. "This is certainly a peculiar situation. I'm not going to rule on the objection for the moment, but I am going to ask this witness some questions myself. Regardless of whether anyone except a close relative is in a position to question the decisions of the Court in a matter of this sort, the Court certainly has the right to be fully advised in the premises."

"We have no objection whatever to a most searching examination by the Court," Melrose said, "but we are simply trying to forestall a long hearing in which a total stranger insinuates herself into litigation where she has no interest and no right."

Judge Ballinger nodded, said to Borden Finchley, "You realized, of course, that your brother had, as you express it, been victimized by this young woman?"

"We thought it was a distinct possibility. We decided to look into it."

"By we, you mean Ralph Exeter and your wife?"

"My wife and I. Ralph Exeter knew nothing about it until after we arrived here."

"And you realized, of course, that this young woman had, in your opinion, so insinuated herself into the affections of your half brother that it was quite possible he would make a will leaving her his entire estate?"

Finchley hesitated, shifted his eyes. "We hadn't really considered that point," he said.

"It had never entered your mind?" Judge Ballinger asked.

"No."

"But you did realize that if you could have a conservator appointed, if you could make it appear to a Court that the subject of the Court's order was incapable of carrying on his own business and was in danger of being influenced by shrewd and designing persons, you could prevent his making a will which would stand up in court?"

"Why, no! That didn't enter our minds."

Perry Mason said to Daphne, "Give me that letter."

She handed him the letter which she had received from Horace Shelby.

Mason said, "I am not entirely certain of my status in the case, Your Honor, and I don't want to interrupt the Court's examination. However, in view of the fact that the witness has stated that he saw this letter which Daphne received in Honolulu, I think it is advisable for the Court to read the letter."

Mason took the letter up to Judge Ballinger.

Judge Ballinger read the letter carefully, then turned to Borden Finchley.

"You say that it hadn't occurred to you that your half brother might make a will disinheriting you?"

Finchley hesitated, then said. "Well . . . no."

"That's right," Judge Ballinger said, "you answered that with a flat 'no' without hesitation a short time ago. You have hesitated now but your answer is still 'no'?"

"That's right."

"You don't want to change that answer?"

"No."

"Yet in this letter which I have in my hand," Judge Ballinger said, "the letter which apparently was sent to Daphne and which letter you stated you read, the writer specifically states that he wants Perry Mason to draw up a will leaving his entire estate to Daphne.

"Now then, Mr. Witness, in view of the fact that you have testified that you saw that letter, do you still insist that the thought never entered your mind that he might make a will disinheriting you?"

"Well, of course, after I saw that letter I realized there was that possibility," Finchley said.

"And it was after you saw that letter that you took steps to have yourself appointed as conservator?"

"Well, I had been thinking about it for a long time and—"

"Just answer the question 'yes' or 'no'," Judge Ballinger said. "It was after you saw that letter that you decided to and did start proceedings to have yourself appointed conservator of Horace Shelby's estate?"

"Yes."

Judge Ballinger frowned, said, "Where is Horace Shelby at the present time?"

"He is in a private sanitarium," Finchley said. "It became necessary to take him there. He is quite disoriented and rather violent and we were simply not in a position to care for him. We felt that he needed professional care."

Finchley pointed to his wife. "My wife is a trained nurse—that is, she was a trained nurse. She has seen many of these cases and she unhesitatingly states that Horace Shelby is suffering from senile dementia."

"That's right," a woman's deep voice boomed, as Elinor Finchley arose. "I'm in a position to verify everything my husband has said."

Judge Ballinger said, "You're not a witness as yet, Mrs. Finchley. You haven't been sworn. I would like to ask you, however, if you saw this letter Horace Shelby had written Daphne?"

"Yes, I saw it."

"Who showed it to you?"

"My husband."

"Before it was put in the envelope?"

"I didn't see it put in the envelope."

"The letter was signed?"

"Yes."

"Folded?"

"I can't remember."

"Your best recollection?"

"I have no recollection."

"What did you do with the letter after reading it?"

"Borden put it back in the env—" She bit the word off.

"In the envelope?" Judge Ballinger asked.

"Yes."

"You had then steamed open the envelope?"

"Yes."

"You put it back in the envelope. Did you mail it?"

"No. We put the envelope back on Horace's desk after he asked what had happened to it. He mailed it himself."

"I haven't time to go into this matter at this present hearing," Judge Ballinger said, "because there is another matter heretofore set which comes on the calendar, but I am going to look into this with great care. This matter is continued until—" He turned to the clerk. "When is the first day that we have—Wait a minute. I understand this case of Johnson versus Peabody is going off calendar. That will give us a half a day tomorrow?"

The clerk nodded.

"I'm continuing this matter until tomorrow at two o'clock," Judge Ballinger said. "At that time I want to have Horace Shelby in court; and, in the meantime, I am going to have him examined by a doctor of my own choosing. What is the private sanitarium where he is now located?"

Finchley hesitated.

"The Goodwill Sanitarium at El Mirar," Darwin Melrose said.

"Very well," Judge Ballinger said. "I'm going to continue the matter until tomorrow afternoon at two o'clock. I want it understood that a physician appointed by the Court will examine Mr. Shelby at the sanitarium. I want Mr. Shelby in court and I want it understood that the Court is not going to rule upon the objection disqualifying Perry Mason from appearing in the matter as attorney for Daphne Shelby—or Daphne Raymond, whatever her name may be—from appearing as an interested party until after I have given the matter further consideration.

"I may state that I will probably rule upon the objection at the conclusion of the hearing tomorrow afternoon, and that I will permit the examination of witnesses by Mr. Perry Mason until the Court has made its ruling.

"It is the offhand impression of the Court that the public is sufficiently a party to inquiries of this sort so that the Court can have the assistance of any interested party or any interested counsel, and in the event the Court decides that Mr. Mason is not entitled to appear and interrogate witnesses on behalf of his client, the Court will probably welcome the services of Mr. Perry Mason as *amicus curiae*.

"The matter is continued until tomorrow afternoon at two o'clock."

Chapter FIVE

Daphne clung to Mason's arm as a drowning person clutches a bit of floating wood.

Borden Finchley gave her a vague smile and stalked out of the courtroom.

Darwin Melrose, walking up to Mason, said, "I didn't like to jerk the rug out from under you, Mason, but it was the only way I could play it."

"You haven't jerked any rug out from under anyone as yet," Mason replied, smiling affably.

He put an arm around Daphne's shoulders. "Come on, Daphne," he said, and led the way into an adjoining witness room.

"You sit down here," he said, "until the others have got out of the courtroom. And after that, you're going to find reporters will be hunting you up—probably the sob-sister type of columnists who like to do the Poor-Little-Rich-Girl articles."

"Mr. Mason, this is absolutely incredible," she said. "My whole world has come crashing down around my ears. Good heavens, do you realize what I've been through the last—"

"I know," Mason said. "I understand, but you're a big girl now; you're out in the world. You'll have to learn to take wallops and to come back fighting. Now, let's take stock of the situation and see where we can start fighting."

"What can we do?" she asked.

"Well," Mason said, "we can check for one thing. Although I feel pretty certain they're sure of their facts or they wouldn't have brought them out in this way. Otherwise, it would have been suicidal."

"I still don't understand it," she said.

"The relatives thought they were going to be disinherited but felt that, if there was no will, they could control the estate.

"So they arranged for a visit, contrived in some way to get left alone with the aged testator, then manipulated things so they could claim his mind was failing, that he needed someone to protect him from shrewd and designing persons. . . . And, of course, the shrewd and designing person they always pick is the person they think is going to be the beneficiary under the will.

"If they can get the Court to appoint a guardian or a conservator, they're that much ahead. If they can't, they have at least established a record so that they can claim undue influence and a lack of testamentary capacity when the will is finally brought up for probate."

"I can't imagine people being like that," Daphne said.

Mason looked at her sharply. "Do you mean you're as innocent as all that?"

"No," she said, "I just can't imagine people being that low—particularly where Uncle Horace was concerned. Uncle Horace is the best, the most bighearted man in the world."

"How did he feel toward Borden Finchley?"

"I don't know, Mr. Mason. I do know that he thought they were staying in the house altogether too long; but then when Uncle Borden suggested that I needed a good rest and a trip somewhere on an ocean steamer, Uncle Horace chimed right in with the idea.

"I know that it meant a lot to him. I know that he knew he would have to put up with a lot of inconveniences, but he wanted me to have the rest and relaxation and have a good time.

"I told you Aunt Elinor had been a nurse, and she told Uncle Horace that I was simply working myself to death and taking altogether too many responsibilities for a young girl—that I should be out having a good time."

"All right," Mason said, "I'm going to scout around and see that the coast is clear of reporters and get you out of here. Don't tell anyone where you are staying and try not to talk with reporters. If you do, tell them that you have no comment to make unless I am present at the time of the interview; that, under instructions from your attorney, you are making no statement.

"Can you do that?"

"Of course I can do that," she said. "It will be easy for me. I just don't want to talk about things, but—I just can't understand how anything like this can take place."

"Our system of justice isn't absolutely perfect," Mason said. "But the case isn't finished yet. They may have letters from your Uncle Horace telling them about your parentage, but those letters are hearsay except for the purpose of impeachment. The courthouse containing your birth records has been destroyed by fire. You just sit tight and keep a good grip on yourself."

She shook her head. "I'm finished," she said, the corners of her mouth drooping. "I'm illegitimate, I'm nobody. I'm going to be forced to go out in the world and try and make a living and I haven't anything to offer. I have no skills. I've been too busy taking care of Uncle Horace to ever learn anything that will help me make a living."

"You type, don't you?" Mason asked.

"Sure," she said, bitterly, "I type, but I don't have any shorthand and I haven't had any experience with taking dictation on any kind of a machine. I just compose the letters and bring them to Uncle Horace to sign. That is, I did compose. I guess those days are all over now."

"You use the touch system?" Mason asked.

"Yes, thank heavens, I taught myself that. I was just using a hunt-and-peck system with two fingers on each hand, and I realized that if I didn't break myself of that habit, I'd never be a really finished typist so I started practicing on the touch system and finally mastered it."

"Well," Mason said, "you're doing all right. You can get a job that will keep you going if you have to and if worse comes to worst."

She said, "The worst has already come. I've been batted around . . ." She suddenly squared her shoulders. "No, I haven't either," she said. "And I'm not going to be a beggar. I'm going to make my own way in the world—but first I'm going to see what I can do for Uncle Horace. I'm not going to let those horrid people manipulate him just any old way they want to."

"That's the spirit," Mason said.

She smiled at him and said, "And I'm *not* going to be a beggar."

Mason said, "You endorsed that check for a hundred and twenty-five thousand dollars when you tried to cash it at the bank?"

She nodded.

"That," Mason said, "leaves you with a hundred-and-twenty-five-thousand-dollar check, endorsed in blank, which may not be too good; and that letter which your uncle sent is evidence that—"

"Mr. Mason," she interrupted, "I just can't believe that he isn't my uncle. Oh, this is terrible, some sort of a nightmare that I'll awaken from."

"It may be at that," Mason said, smiling reassuringly. "My experience has always been that these things look much worse than they actually are. In fact, I tell my clients that nine times out of ten they can say to themselves, 'Things are never as bad as they seem.' "

"Thank you for trying to reassure me but I just don't know what to do next. How am I going to live until I can get a job? How can I go and get a room and—

"No, no," she interposed hastily, as Mason started to speak, "don't tell me that you'll finance me. I can't just live on your charity."

"It isn't charity," Mason said. "It's a business investment. Give me that check and the letter. I'm going to keep them in my office safe."

She said, "That letter, I'm afraid, shows that Uncle Horace or should I say Mr. Shelby—never made a will in my favor and suddenly realized that he hadn't made a will."

"Don't be too sure," Mason said. "Many times a person makes a will entirely in his own handwriting—which is perfectly legal and valid—but then wants to have it supplemented by another will executed in the presence of witnesses."

"A will in handwriting is good without witnesses?" she asked.

"In this state, yes," Mason said. "The holographic will, entirely written, dated and signed by the testator, is valid.

"There are, of course, several catches or legal pitfalls. There can't be anything on the sheet of paper except the handwriting of the testator. In other words, if part of the date is printed and the testator only has to fill in the day and month, then the will is considered as not being entirely of the handwriting of the testator. The testator should start with an absolutely blank piece of paper on which there is no writing or printing of any sort. He should set forth that he is making a will. He should be sure to state the date. He should make a clear disposition of his property and sign it. Now, I have a feeling that your Uncle Horace, being a pretty shrewd businessman, did make such a will."

"But if they are in charge of his papers, they can find it and destroy it," she said. "Probably they have already done that."

Mason shrugged his shoulders. "I can't answer that as yet. It is always a possibility. However, remember that we have seriously impeached Borden Finchley by this letter; having sworn that he had no thought about the possibility of his half brother executing a will which would disinherit him; and then having admitted he had seen this letter, he put himself in a very questionable position.

"You could see Judge Ballinger turn against him the minute he made that statement.

"Well, Daphne, I admit things look black, but we're going to keep fighting; and don't you get discouraged. . . . You have enough money for your present needs?"

She nodded. "Thanks to your generosity," she said.

"It's all right," he told her. "I repeat, I'm just putting up a little money as an investment. After I collect some money for you, you can repay me and pay me a fee as well."

Her smile was wan. "I am afraid that your chances of getting a good fee are just about as slim as your chances of ever getting repaid. I suppose after I get a job I can pay you ten or fifteen dollars a month—something like that."

Mason patted her shoulder. "Let me give you some good advice, Daphne. Quit worrying about the future."

Mason left her and went to his office, fitted his latchkey to the door of his private office, and shook his head at Della Street.

"The poor kid," he said. "I felt so sorry for her—her whole world crashing about her ears."

"What chances does she have?" Della Street asked.

"I don't know," Mason said. "If we can get the order appointing a conservator set aside and if Horace Shelby is the type of man I think he is, we can do some good. But remember that Horace Shelby has been through a whole series of devastating experiences and these have probably been complicated by some medication which is contra-indicated in his condition. There may be some permanent damage there.

"You can see their strategy," Mason went on. "They got rid of Daphne for the longest possible period of time. While she was gone, they did everything they could to undermine the mental health of Horace Shelby. Then when they didn't dare to wait any longer, they went to court. Of course, the fact that he was trying to give his niece—who it now seems is actually a stranger to the blood—one hundred and twenty-five thousand dollars, which virtually wiped out his checking account, was a big factor in the mind of the Court.

"You put yourself in the position of a judge and find a set of circumstances like that and you're pretty certain to feel that the man needs protection."

Della Street nodded, said, "Mr. Stanley Paxton is waiting in the office for you."

Mason nodded. "Let's have him in," he said. "In the meantime, Della, remember that I have this check for one hundred and twenty-five thousand dollars made to Daphne Shelby and endorsed by her, and also the letter that Horace Shelby sent her. I want to put them in our safe and I'd like to have a photographer make photographic copies of them."

Della Street reached out her hand.

"I'll keep them for the moment," Mason said. "Let's not delay seeing Mr. Paxton. His time is valuable."

Della Street went to the outer office, returned with Stanley Paxton.

"Mr. Mason," the banker said, "I find myself in a peculiar situation."

Mason raised his eyebrows in silent inquiry as he gestured to a chair.

Paxton seated himself, ran his hand over his high forehead, looked shrewdly at Mason and said, "We have had a little experience in these matters from time to time and we can size people up. Our primary interest as a bank is in protecting our clients."

Mason nodded.

"Horace Shelby is our client," Paxton went on. "As far as we are concerned, the conservator is a stranger—an intruder, an interloper."

"Under an order of Court," Mason pointed out.

"Under an order of Court, to be sure," Paxton conceded. "That's what I want to talk with you about."

Mason nodded. "Go right ahead."

"Of course, it's unusual because you are attorney—not for Horace Shelby but for his niece."

Mason was silent, waiting for the other to continue.

Paxton put the tips of his fingers together, looked steadily at a spot on the floor about five feet in front of him. He spoke in the tone of voice used by a man who is accustomed to dealing in precise figures and wants to express himself in such a way that he conveys exactly the thought he wants to convey.

"In dealing with the conservator," Paxton said, "the general custom is for the conservator to file with us a certified copy of the order of Court and have us transfer the account to the conservator."

"That custom wasn't followed in the present case?" Mason asked.

"In the present case," Paxton said, "I remember the wording of the Court order very clearly because I have had occasion to look it up. It said that Borden Finchley, as conservator, was to take possession of all funds on deposit in the Investors National Bank in the name of Horace Shelby, and safeguard those funds as conservator. An order was made to the bank ordering the bank to turn over every credit existing in the bank as of the date of that order to the conservator.

"Then Borden Finchley—apparently not trusting us—drew a check on us for the exact amount of the balance on hand in the account of Horace Shelby."

"And opened a new account as conservator?" Mason asked.

"He did that temporarily. He opened a new account as conservator but, within two hours, went to another bank, opened an account in the name of Borden Finchley, conservator for the estate of Horace Shelby, and cleaned out the account."

Mason grinned. "He evidently didn't want to antagonize you until you had transferred the money to his account, then he went out of his way to give you a deliberate slap in the face."

"Probably," Paxton said, "he realized that our attitude was somewhat unsympathetic. We considered Horace Shelby a rather elderly but very shrewd individual. Some people are old at seventy-five, some people are alert at ninety."

"And Horace Shelby was mentally alert?"

"We considered him a very lovable old gentleman. I'll be frank with you, Mr. Mason, he would get a little confused at times and he knew it, and he relied implicitly on Daphne."

"And what's your opinion of Daphne?"

"She's a jewel. She's just a sweet, loyal girl who sacrificed her entire life for her uncle; and she did it out of affection and not because she was looking to see which side of the bread had the butter."

Mason nodded, said after a moment, "Well, the money was taken over under a Court order and it's out of the bank."

"That is true," Paxton said. "It might have been better if Finchley had handled it in the ordinary way and simply taken over everything in Shelby's account at the bank and served us with an order that only the signature of the conservator was to be recognized."

"What do you mean?" Mason asked.

"Simply this," Paxton said. "Yesterday afternoon a deposit of fifty thousand dollars was made to the credit of Horace Shelby."

"What?" Mason exclaimed.

Paxton nodded. "It was a payment due under a contract of purchase," he said, "and the contract provided that the money could be paid by depositing it to the credit of Horace Shelby in our bank. A grant deed had already been executed by Horace Shelby and placed in escrow with a title company with instructions that whenever the purchaser showed a deposit slip showing that the final fifty thousand dollars had been paid to the account of Horace Shelby at our bank, the deed was to be delivered.

"The purchaser knew nothing of the appointment of a conservator and insisted on depositing the money to the account of Horace Shelby and receiving a duplicate deposit slip, which he took to the escrow company."

Mason pursed his lips.

"Now then," Paxton went on, "we are in a peculiar situation. If we notify Borden Finchley of this extra fifty thousand dollars, he will simply have another order prepared and have that account transferred to his name. But do we need to notify him?"

"Certainly," Mason said. "I think it's your duty to notify him."

Paxton's face showed his disappointment.

"You should write him a letter immediately," Mason said, "and explain the circumstances to him."

Paxton got to his feet. "Well," he said, his manner showing disappointment, "I was hoping that perhaps you could suggest some other means of handling it."

Mason shook his head. "That's the only ethical thing to do," he said. "Go to the bank and write a letter. In fact, I'll walk down to the bank with you. I have some business in that direction. We can walk together."

"If Horace Shelby knew about this money," Paxton said, "I think he'd contrive in some way to take care of Daphne."

"There's nothing he can do," Mason said. "Your attorney would advise you that you couldn't take chances."

"Yes, I suppose so," Paxton said, with a sigh. "But you have the reputation of being very ingenious, Mr. Mason, and I thought I'd let you know."

"I'm glad you did," Mason said. "The bank's only a few doors down the street, I'll go on down with you."

"And you feel I should write Borden Finchley a letter?"

"Immediately," Mason said.

They walked down to the elevator, then strolled down the street. Paxton seemed to be dragging his feet.

"Of course," Paxton pointed out, "you can see what Shelby was trying to do. He was *trying* to care of Daphne financially. That's what *he* wanted. If he hadn't been so anxious to take care of her, the Court might have been more hesitant about appointing a conservator."

"I suppose so," Mason said. "How's my credit at your bank, by the way?"

"*Your* credit?" Paxton asked in surprise. "Why, absolutely A-1."

"I'd like to borrow seventy-five thousand dollars," Mason said.

"Why, I think that can be arranged. You have some security?"

"No security," Mason said. "I would give my note."

Paxton started to shake his head, then frowned. "How long would you want the money, Mr. Mason?"

"About ten minutes," Mason said.

Paxton looked at him incredulously. "Seventy-five thousand dollars for ten minutes?"

"Yes," Mason said.

"Good heavens, what do you intend to do with it?"

Mason grinned. "I thought I would deposit it to the account of Horace Shelby."

"Are you crazy?" Paxton asked. "Are you . . ." Suddenly he stopped dead in his tracks, regarded Mason in a bewildered manner, then broke out laughing.

"Come on," he said, "let's get to the bank just as fast as we can."

He started walking more rapidly, and Mason lengthened his strides to keep up with the banker.

They entered the bank. Paxton called in a secretary. He said, "If you don't mind, Mr. Mason, I'll dictate a letter to Borden Finchley telling him—"

"I think," Mason interrupted, "the better procedure would be to make the letter to Horace Shelby, care of Borden Finchley, Conservator."

Paxton grinned. "I get the point," he said. "It's a legal distinction, but an important one."

Paxton turned to the secretary. "Take a letter to Horace Shelby, care of Borden Finchley, Conservator.

"Dear Mr. Shelby, The fifty thousand dollar final payment on the purchase of the Broadway property was deposited to your account by the purchaser, who took a duplicate deposit slip to deliver to the escrow department. Paragraph. That money is now on deposit in your name. Very truly yours, etc."

Mason nodded. "Now," he said, "could we visit the Loan Department?"

"Right away," Paxton said.

Paxton went on, "I think, Mr. Mason, under the circumstances, I'll okay this loan myself. You want seventy-five thousand dollars?"

Mason nodded.

"I'll make it for thirty days," Paxton said.

"Any time you like," Mason said. "I won't want it that long but if you'd like to have your records to show, why, it will be for that period."

Paxton made out the note. Mason signed it.

"How do you want this?" Paxton asked.

Mason said, "I think, under the circumstances, cash would be preferable—seventy-five one-thousand-dollar bills."

Paxton went to the vault and returned with the seventy-five one-thousand-dollar bills.

"I think," he said to Mason, "that from here on you had better handle this through regular channels."

"Exactly," Mason said, and shook hands.

Mason put the money in his pocket, walked out to the window of a teller, made out duplicate deposit slips, and shuffled his way along in the line of customers.

When he reached the window, he pulled out the seventy-five one-thousand-dollar bills and the duplicate deposit slip.

"Please deposit this to the account of Horace Shelby," he said.

The teller looked at the seventy-five thousand dollars in surprise. "A cash deposit for seventy-five thousand dollars?" he asked.

"Exactly," Mason said.

"I think that account has been transferred," the teller said. "I'm sorry but—"

"Can't the bank take a deposit?"

"Yes, I guess we could."

"Then, please deposit this to the account of Horace Shelby."

The teller said, "Just a moment. I'm going to have to ask someone about this."

He was gone a few minutes, then returned and said, "If you insist on making the deposit, Mr. Mason, we have no alternative but to accept it."

"Very well," Mason said. "I want to make the deposit."

The teller stamped and signed the duplicate deposit slips.

"Now then," Mason said, taking the endorsed check of Daphne Shelby from his pocket, "I have a check here that I would like to cash. A check for a hundred and twenty-five thousand dollars."

"You want to *cash* a check for one hundred and twenty-five thousand dollars?" the teller asked.

"That's right," Mason said, and handed the check through the window.

The teller looked at the check in frowning incredulity then, suddenly, a light dawned on his face.

"Just a minute," he said. "I'll also have to check on this."

He left the window and was back in a few moments. "It happens," he said, "that there is just enough money in the account to pay this check."

"I'm not interested in the amount of the account," Mason said. "I only want to cash the check."

The teller said, "This is a most unusual situation, Mr. Mason."

Mason yawned. "Perhaps it's unusual for you," he said, and glanced significantly at his wrist watch.

The teller said, "How do you want this, Mr. Mason?"

"In thousand-dollar bills," Mason said.

The teller opened his drawer, carefully counted out the seventy-five thousand that Mason had deposited, then counted out twenty thousand more bills, summoned the messenger to go to the vault, said, "Just a moment, please," and, a few minutes later, handed Mason the balance of the money in thousand-dollar bills.

"Thank you," Mason said.

He put the money in his pocket, walked over to the enclosure in which Stanley Paxton had his desk and said, "Mr. Paxton, I borrowed seventy-five thousand dollars from the bank a short time ago."

"Yes, indeed," Paxton said. "It was a short-term thirty-day note on your personal security, Mr. Mason."

"Exactly," Mason said.

"I find that I have no further use for the money," Mason said, "and would like to pay off the note."

"Why, that's most unusual!" Paxton said.

"I know it is," Mason said. "As I figure the interest for one day, it amounts to about twelve dollars and thirty-two cents."

The lawyer gravely put seventy-five thousand-dollar bills, a ten-dollar bill, two one-dollar bills, and thirty-two cents on the banker's desk.

"Well, this is most unusual!" Paxton said. "However, if you insist on paying off the note, I guess we have no alternative but to accept it. Just a moment, please." Paxton took the money, put it in the drawer of his desk, picked up an interoffice telephone and said, "Send me in the Perry Mason note for seventy-five thousand dollars please. Mark it 'Paid' . . . That's right, I know it just came in . . . That's right. *Mark it 'Paid'!*"

After some three minutes, a young man approached the desk with the promissory note.

"Here you are," Paxton said. "I'm sorry you didn't have further use for the money. We like to put our money out at interest on a good security."

"Oh, I understand," Mason said. "Now, I have one other request. I have fifty thousand dollars in cash. I would like to buy ten cashier's checks for five thousand dollars each, payable to Daphne Shelby. I believe you are acquainted with Miss Shelby."

"Oh, yes, " Paxton said, we know her quite well. She does all the business for her uncle. You wanted ten cashier's checks of five thousand dollars each?"

"That's right."

"If you can wait for just a few more minutes," Paxton said.

He took the fifty thousand dollars, left his desk and within a matter of fifteen minutes returned with the ten cashier's checks.

"Thank you very much," Mason said.

The banker stood up.

"I've shaken hands with you once, Mr. Mason," he said. "I'm going to shake hands with you again, and I hope you'll forgive me for my momentary doubts as to your ingenuity. When I really violated a confidence to give you information in your office, I was hoping against hope that you'd find some way of handling the matter, and then I felt my hopes dashed to the ground. I realize now that I should have had more confidence."

The banker gripped the lawyer's hand firmly, then patted him on the shoulder. "Good luck, Mr. Mason," he said.

"Thanks very much," Mason said. "And thanks to the Investors National Bank for the interest it takes in its clients. I can assure you that this action will eventually rebound to your benefit."

"Thank you. Thank you very much," Paxton said.

The lawyer, with the ten cashier's checks in his inside pocket, left the bank, went to Daphne Shelby's hotel.

"Daphne," he said when he confronted the young woman, "you're no longer a beautiful beggar."

"What do you mean?" she asked.

Mason took the ten cashier's checks from his pocket.

She looked at each one incredulously. "What in the world!" she asked.

Mason said, "Just endorse this one check 'Pay to the order of Perry Mason.' "

"That's your fee?" she asked.

"We're not talking about a fee yet," Mason said. "I'm having you endorse this so I can get five thousand dollars in cash and send it over to you. That's all you should have on your person at the present time. In fact, you'd better get traveler's checks for about forty-five hundred dollars with it. The other checks you should hold against a rainy day."

Chapter SIX

Mason had been back in his office less than an hour when Paul Drake's code knock sounded on the door.

Della Street admitted the detective and Drake said, "Well, I've got Ralph Exeter pegged."

"What about him?" Mason asked.

Drake said, "Exeter's real name is Cameron. His first name is a queer one—Bosley, B-O-S-L-E-Y. He's from Las Vegas. He's a gambler, and he's holding Borden Finchley's IOUs for over a hundred and fifty thousand bucks."

"So that explains a lot," Mason said.

"There's more to it than that," Drake went on. "Cameron became involved himself and, until he can get the money on those IOUs of Finchley, Cameron can't get back in good standing with his own crowd. So Cameron is hiding out. That's why he has taken the name of Ralph Exeter of Boston, Massachusetts."

Mason said, "That's darned good work, Paul. You did a wonderful job."

Drake shook his head and said, "I didn't really do anything. I just happened to cross the back trail of people who are trying to find Cameron."

"How?"

"Well, it was just a combination of circumstances. Finchley gave a rather synthetic background of where he had been and what he had been doing, but the person that comes in to do the housecleaning noticed that there were Las Vegas stickers on his baggage when he first came there, and that Finchley was at great pains to scrub them off the second day he was there.

"You remember Finchley said they were driving in Exeter's car. I traced the license plates on Exeter's car. They were Massachusetts license plates all right, but I used the long distance telephone, got some quick action, and found the person who was registered as owning that car when it left Massachusetts.

"He went to Las Vegas, became involved in a gambling game, and this man Cameron, to whom he owed a little over a thousand dollars, offered to trade automobiles and give him the difference. The fellow had no alternative but to make the deal so they simply traded possession of the cars without going through the formality of getting registrations transferred. They felt they could do that later on when they applied for new licenses.

"Once I had that lead, I did a little telephoning in Las Vegas and found that Cameron was one of those big-shot gamblers who will be way up in the clouds one day and way down in the depths the next.

"He got wiped out in a poker game and had some IOUs floating around. He told friends that he had a pigeon who owed him a hundred and fifty grand and that the pigeon had it all made, but it was going to take a little while to cash in; that he was going to ride herd on his pigeon until the money came in.

"Then Cameron disappeared.

"At first, the people who held Cameron's paper were willing to wait but now they're getting a little restless and they'd like very much to know where Cameron is."

Mason grinned, said, "Now then, Paul, we're beginning to get someplace. This is the sort of ammunition we can shoot."

"It's a shame we didn't have it for the hearing," Drake said.

"We'll have it for the next round," Mason told him.

The phone rang.

Della Street answered it, then looked inquiringly at Mason. "Will you talk with Mr. Darwin Melrose?" she asked.

"Certainly," Mason said, and picked up the telephone. "Hello, Melrose. What can I do for you?"

Melrose was so excited he talked with machine-gun rapidity. "What the devil have you been up to? The title company tells me that an escrow was terminated, that a man made a final payment on property to Horace Shelby—a payment of fifty thousand dollars."

"Yes?" Mason asked as Melrose stopped for breath.

"So we get at the Investors National and they said there wasn't any money in the Shelby account. We asked them about that fifty-thousand-dollar deposit and they said it had all been checked out, that there had been two deposits made—one of fifty thousand and one of seventy-five thousand, and they had a canceled check payable to Daphne Shelby for one hundred and twenty-five thousand, which had wiped the account out."

"Why, that's right," Mason said. "There's no secret about that. We discussed that check in court. Your own client knew all about it."

"Knowing about the check is one thing; getting it cashed is another."

"Well," Mason said, "the check was left in the possession of Daphne Shelby. There was money in the bank to cover the check. The bank had a right to cash it and she had a right to present it."

"But the bank knew a conservator had been appointed."

"The bank had been advised that a conservator had been appointed for the account of Horace Shelby as the account stood at that time. Nothing was said about any future accounts or any future deposits."

"Well, we didn't think it was necessary since we were cleaning out the entire account."

"I'm sorry if you misunderstood the situation," Mason said. "But your order to the bank was very specific. It was ordered to turn over to the conservator the exact amount that was on deposit in Shelby's account at the date the order was served."

"I don't like this," Melrose said. "I don't think the Court is going to like it either. It's sharp practice."

"I beg your pardon!" Mason said.

"I said it was sharp practice."

"I think you misunderstood the situation," Mason said with a grin. "It wasn't sharp practice on my side; it was dull practice on yours.

Go into court, if you want to, and see what the judge has to say about it."

"That's exactly what I intend to do," Melrose said. "I'm going to ask the judge to make an order to show cause why you shouldn't be found guilty of contempt of Court and an order demanding that you turn all of the money you received on that check over to the conservator."

"That's certainly your privilege," Mason said. "Go ahead and make the motions in court and I'll be there to answer them. . . . Was there anything else you had in mind?"

Instead of answering the question, Darwin Melrose slammed the telephone back in place.

Mason grinned at Paul Drake and said, "You know, Paul, it's a long worm that has no turning."

Drake said, "I gather from your conversation that you slipped over a fast one?"

"Well, I don't know," Mason said judicially. "Darwin Melrose is one of those attorneys who wants to be specific. If he wants to describe a horse with a white, right hind leg, he makes the description read 'a horse with *one* white, right hind leg.'

"Of course, he knew just what the balance was in Shelby's account, so he made the order which he served on the bank specific— that they were to turn over to the conservator Shelby's account consisting of exactly so many thousand dollars, so many hundred dollars and so many cents—right around a hundred and fifty-six thousand dollars.

"Of course, it never occured to him that someone might make a deposit in Shelby's name."

"And someone did?" Drake asked.

"Someone did," Mason said.

"Did you have anything to do with it?"

"Oh a little," Mason admitted, with a grin. "We have carried out Horace Shelby's wishes in part and, thanks to the information you have, we may be able to carry the amount the rest of the way."

"Your client?" Drake asked. "I take it you've seen she's provided for?"

"She's provided for."

"Don't you think she's a little bit too naïve?" Drake asked.

"What do you mean?"

"For a girl who's been handling her uncle's business affairs, writing all of his correspondence, more or less doing his thinking for him in matters running into a good many thousands of dollars, she seems just a little bit synthetic in her unsophistication."

Mason regarded the detective with thoughtful eyes. "You know, Paul, I've been thinking the same thing. I've been wondering if back of that schoolgirl naïve character there isn't a pretty smart mind. But remember, the bank has been doing business with her for a long time. They've known the connection between her and her uncle and they're for her all the way."

"Oh, I think she's all right," Drake said, "but—I don't know. Do you suppose she's suspected the true relationship and just kept playing demure so that Horace Shelby would never know she suspected?"

Mason shrugged his shoulders. "I'm darned if I know, Paul. But —What do you think, Della?"

Della shook her head. "You don't get me to express my opinion," she said.

"You have one?"

"Yes."

"And why don't you want to express it?"

"I'm not sure of my grounds," she said thoughtfully.

"Well," Mason said, "we're doing the best we can for her. She's had a whole series of jolts but I think, in the long run, we're going to come out all right.

"Who's the doctor the Court is appointing, Paul?"

"I don't know as yet," Drake said, "but I've got a line out so I can find out just as soon as—" He was interrupted by the telephone.

Della Street picked up the phone, said, "It's for you, Paul. Your office is calling on the unlisted line."

Drake took the call, said, "Give me that name again," said, "thanks," hung up and turned to Perry Mason. "Okay, Perry," he said, "the question is answered. The Court has appointed Dr. Grantland Alma as the Court's doctor."

Della Street immediately started riffling through the pages of the phone book, then furnished the supplemental information. "Here he is," she said. "His office is 602 Center Building and his phone is Lavine 2-3681."

"And," Mason said, "any attempt to influence him will make him mad but there's no reason why I, as an attorney, can't try to see Horace Shelby before the doctor does."

"You stand absolutely no chance," Paul Drake said.

Mason grinned. "If they've got him shut off from all of his friends, it might be a good thing to know."

The lawyer looked at his watch. "It's a cinch the doctor is in his office now. He probably won't try to see Shelby until tomorrow morning. Give his nurse a ring, Della."

"The nurse?"

"Yes. One should always communicate with a doctor through his nurse."

Della Street put through the call and nodded to Mason.

Mason said, "Hello, this is Perry Mason, the attorney, talking and I would like very much to talk with Dr. Alma on the telephone. If that is not possible, I would like to ask a question which he could answer. It is a matter of some urgency."

The feminine voice at the other end of the line said, "Well, this is his nurse. Perhaps you'd better give me the question. The doctor is busy now and has an office full of patients."

Mason said, "Dr. Alma, who's been appointed by Judge Ballinger to examine Horace Shelby sometime before a court hearing which is to take place—"

"Oh, I'm sure the doctor wouldn't discuss that with you or with anyone," the nurse said.

"I don't want him to," Mason said. "I am simply trying to find out if it would interfere with the doctor's plans in any way if I went out to the Goodwill Sanitarium to visit Mr. Shelby."

"Oh, I'm sure it wouldn't," the nurse said. "Just so you don't do anything to upset him or alarm him. You're one of the attorneys in the case?"

"In the general case, yes," Mason said.

"Just be careful not to disturb him in case he should be excitable."

"Thank you," Mason said. "What room is he in, by the way?"

"He's in one of the isolation units, I believe. Just a minute . . . Unit 17."

"Thank you very much," Mason said.

"You're entirely welcome."

"Please tell Dr. Alma I called."

"I will."

"Well," Mason said, grinning as he hung up the phone, "if you want information, the way to go about it is to get it openly."

Drake grinned. "A good private detective could have put in two days at fifty dollars a day getting you that information, Perry. . . . You want me to go with you?"

"No," Mason said, "I think I'll go alone."

"The party may get rough out there," Drake warned.

"Under proper circumstances," Mason said, "I have been known to get rough myself."

Chapter SEVEN

The Goodwill Sanitarium and Rest Home at El Mirar was apparently the combination of a reconverted motel and a large old-fashioned three-story dwelling on an adjoining lot.

The properties had been united, a board fence put around the property, and on the windows of the motel units as well as on the windows on the lower floor of the big building were unobtrusive iron work—either ornamental grillwork or straight rectangular bars.

Perry Mason sized up the property, then made no effort to be surreptitious but walked through the gate, up the wide driveway and through the front door where a sign said OFFICE.

The lawyer noticed a sign on the gate reading, "Wanted: Young, well-adjusted woman with agreeable personality for general work." There was a similar sign in a frame on the side of the office door. Since these signs had been hand-lettered by a professional, it was apparent that the institution had quite a turnover in domestic help and experienced considerable trouble in getting replacements.

Mason entered the office.

There was a long counter across the room dividing it into two parts. Behind this counter was a switchboard and a chair; to one side, a desk littered with papers, a tilting swivel chair, two straight-backed swivel chairs; and a shelf of square cubbyholes, with room numbers over each partition.

A light was on at the switchboard and there was the customary loud buzzing sound indicating an incoming call.

Mason walked to the counter.

A middle-aged woman came hurrying through a door which opened from the back of the office. She hardly looked at Mason but went to the switchboard, picked up the headset and said, "Yes. Hello. This is the Goodwill Sanitarium."

She listened for a minute, then said, "Well, he isn't in now. I've left word with his secretary. He'll call as soon as he gets back. . . . No, I don't know just when he'll be back. . . . Yes, I hope so. Yes, sometime today. . . . Yes, he'll call you, Doctor. As soon as he gets back, he'll call. . . . Goodbye."

She pulled out the plug, turned wearily and somewhat truculently to the counter.

"What can I do for *you?*" she asked Mason.

"You have a Horace Shelby here," Mason said.

Instantly the woman stiffened. Her eyes grew wary.

"What about it?" she asked.

"I want to see him," Mason said.

"You a relative?"

"I'm a lawyer."

"You representing him?"

"I'm representing a relative."

"It's past visiting hours today," she said.

"But it's rather important that I see him," Mason said.

She shook her head firmly. "You have to come during visiting hours."

"And when are they?"

"Two to three in the afternoon."

"You mean I can't see him until tomorrow afternoon?"

"I'm not certain you can see him then. You're going to have to talk to Doctor. He's been having a little trouble. There's been a 'No Visitors' sign on his door . . . What did you say your name was?"

"Mason. Perry Mason."

"I'll tell Doctor you called."

"Doctor who?" Mason asked.

"Doctor Baxter," she said. "Tillman Baxter. He runs the place."

"He's a medical doctor?" Mason asked.

"He has a license to run the place," she said. "That's all I know and I don't think it's going to do you any good to come back. I don't think Horace Shelby is going to be in any condition to receive visitors."

She abruptly turned her back on him and walked through the door leading from the office into the back room.

Mason turned away, made a quick survey of the place, and walked back to where he had parked his car.

A man was standing by the car. "You're the Court-appointed doctor?" the man asked.

Mason regarded the man thoughtfully. "What Court-appointed doctor?" he asked.

"The Shelby case."

"Why?" Mason asked.

"I want to talk with you," the man said.

"May I ask what about?"

"You didn't answer my question. Are you the Court-appointed doctor?"

"No," Mason said. "I'm Perry Mason, an attorney. Now why did you want to talk with the—"

The man didn't wait for him to finish the sentence, but walked rapidly to a car which was parked ahead of Mason's, jumped in, said something to the driver of the car, and the car took off down the street.

Mason tried to make out the license number but the car had been parked too far ahead. He could see that it was a Nevada license and that was all.

The lawyer pretended to return to the sanitarium, but doubled back and, pulling the key for his own car from his pocket, hurried around to the street side to jump in behind the wheel. He started the motor and drove rapidly down the street.

He didn't see the car with the Nevada license plates. It had evidently turned off to one of the side streets.

The lawyer drove around several blocks trying to spot the car so he could get the license number but was unable to find it.

He drove back to his office.

"There's a call from Dr. Alma," Della Street told him. "He says he'll talk with you any time that you come in. I told him I expected you shortly."

Mason nodded.

"Gertie's closed up the office and gone home," Della Street said. "I'll put the call through."

Her fingers were a blur of motion over the dial on the telephone and she said, "Dr. Alma, please. Mr. Mason calling."

She nodded to Perry Mason.

Mason picked up the telephone. "Hello," he said, "Perry Mason talking."

"Dr. Grantland Alma, Mason. You wanted to talk with me?"

"Yes. I understand you've been appointed by Judge Ballinger to talk with Horace Shelby and make an appraisal of his physical and mental condition."

"That's right."

"Do you expect to see Horace Shelby soon?"

"I can't see him before tomorrow morning," Dr. Alma said, "but I have told the sanitarium I'll be there at ten o'clock in the morning."

"Is it wise to let them know exactly when you'll be there?" Mason asked.

"I think so," Dr. Alma said, "because I've told them that I want him to have no sedation after eight o'clock tonight; that I want a complete chart showing every bit of medication that has been given and that I don't want anyone from the sanitarium present when I examine him; that I'll have my own nurse with me."

Mason grinned and said, "Thank you, Doctor. I can see why the Court decided to appoint you as the examining physician. . . . I just wanted to ask you if ample precautions would be taken to see that the patient had a fair chance."

Dr. Alma said, "I know what you're thinking. I may also tell you that there are certain sedatives which, when given intravenously, put a patient into a deep sleep; but in some cases the individual becomes disoriented and a little erratic for several days. There are also other drugs which, when given to a person who has arteriosclerosis, can cause quite a bit of mental impairment."

"Can you test for those drugs?"

"Yes and no. I can make a blood test which will be of some help if

I think they have been administered, but I can pretty well tell whether a person is his normal self or whether he is recuperating from the influence of drugs.

"I know all about you and your reputation, Mr. Mason. I understand you're representing the niece or the young woman who thought she was the niece—in any event, the young woman who's been taking care of the patient and who has been very devoted to him. I can also tell you in confidence that the sanitarium gave me an argument when I said I didn't want any medication after eight tonight. They told me the patient was restless, highly irritable, unable to sleep, and that he would have to be given heavy sedation.

"I asked what they meant by heavy sedation and we had an argument over that. I finally gave them a limit of a sleeping medicine that could be given the patient tonight.

"I don't mind telling you, Mr. Mason, that I'm going to check this thing carefully. That's what I was told to do and that's what I'm going to do."

"Thanks a lot," Mason said. "I just wanted to find out what you had in mind."

"And I think I know what you have in mind," Dr. Alma said, chuckling. "Don't worry, Mason, I'm going to be fair but I'm going to be very, very thorough."

"Thanks a lot," Mason said. "And I certainly appreciate your co-operation."

The lawyer hung up and said to Della Street, "I guess there's no reason we can't close the office and go home. I think everything is taken care of. Dr. Alma knows what he's doing. He evidently knows all of the angles. Daphne is out of circulation. The sanitarium is on the defensive and I wouldn't be too surprised if tomorrow was a day with plenty of action, as far as the sanitarium is concerned."

"How did it impress you?" she asked.

Mason made a gesture with his hand. "It's one of those things," he said. "I think the man they call 'Doctor' who is in charge of it is not a licensed physician although he probably has a license to run a nursing home.

"Some of those places are all right; some of them aren't. In fact, in some of them—heaven help the poor guy who gets put in there! All too frequently, relatives don't want to be bothered with an old man who is getting a little forgetful and a little unsanitary in his habits, so they bundle him off to a nursing home, wash their hands of him, and practically forget about him.

"The nursing home doesn't care just as long as they get a regular monthly check.

"Then there are some of those nursing homes which are pretty foxy. They know when the old man is supposed to be incompetent; and when they know the patient hates them, but the person who has been appointed guardian or conservator of the estate is making the check every month, it doesn't take long for them to decide which side of the bread has the butter."

"And you think this sanitarium is one of those places?"

Mason said, "I wouldn't be the least surprised, Della. However I think things are working all right now. Let's call it a day and go home."

Chapter EIGHT

Perry Mason entered the office at nine o'clock the following morning to find Della Street opening mail and segregating it into three piles: Urgent, Important, and Unimportant.

Mason casually glanced through some of the letters on the Urgent pile, said, "Well, I guess we may as well do a little catching up, Della. . . . Have you heard anything from Daphne?"

"Not yet."

Mason glanced at his watch. "In an hour, Dr. Alma will be out at the sanitarium to examine Horace Shelby. I imagine there'll be some action about that time."

"What sort of action?" Della asked.

"I don't know," Mason said. "Several things are possible. Either they've drugged the old man, ignoring Dr. Alma's orders; or they'll try to invent some reason why Dr. Alma can't see him."

"And what will Dr. Alma do?" Della Street asked.

"From the way he talked," Mason said, "I imagine he'll tell the sanitarium people he's going to see Horace Shelby or they're going to be hauled into court for contempt."

"And if he's drugged?" she asked.

"Dr. Alma will find it out and so report to the Court."

"And if he isn't?"

"If he isn't," Mason said, "I'm betting ten to one that Horace Shelby is as bright as a dollar. Probably rather the worse for wear as a result of his experience but he'll be logical and coherent and I think we'll get the Court's order appointing a conservator set aside. And the minute that happens, Shelby will order the Finchleys out of his house, make a will in favor of Daphne Shelby, and everything will end happily."

"What about the business you did of cashing the check? Won't they make trouble over that?"

"They'll try to," Mason said, "but my best guess is that they're going to have their hands full with other things. In a matter of this sort, the best defense is a counteroffensive. . . . All right, let's get some of these letters out of the way."

The lawyer dictated until ten o'clock, then stretched and yawned.

"That's enough for the time being, Della. I can't get my mind off the Goodwill Sanitarium and what's apt to be happening out there. . . . Give Daphne a ring. Let's tell her to stand by. There's just a chance the whole opposition may collapse."

"You're optimistic this morning," Della Street said, reaching for the telephone.

"Had a wonderful night's sleep," Mason said, grinning, "a good breakfast, and— Hang it, Della, just the way Dr. Alma talked over the telephone made me feel that he knows what he's doing. The minute a doctor of that caliber who knows what he's doing enters a case of this kind he strikes confusion into the other side.

"If the so-called sanitarium and rest home is in danger of losing its license or thinks it is, they're very apt to swing right around to the other extreme."

Della said into the telephone, "Miss Daphne Shelby, please. She's in Room 718."

She held the phone for a while, then frowned, looked at her watch and said to Mason, "There's no answer."

"All right," Mason said, as Della waited, "leave a message for her. Tell her to call Mr. Mason when she comes in."

Della duly transmitted the message, then hung up the telephone.

"I have an idea she slept late and is in the dining room eating breakfast," Mason said.

"Or perhaps out shopping," Della said. "After all, she came into quite a windfall, thanks to your financial skulduggery."

"No skulduggery about it," Mason said, grinning. "Darwin Melrose is the kind of attorney who goes into so darned much detail he sometimes lets the general issue slip through his fingers.

"Melrose was so specific about the fact that the exact amount of the balance which was in the account that day was to be turned over to Borden Finchley, as the conservator, that he entirely forgot to mention that the Court had appointed Finchley as conservator of all of Horace Shelby's property; and that any accounts, credits, or other tangibles which the bank held in its possession or which might come into its possession were to be turned over to the conservator. He simply made a specific demand for that one account and then had Finchley check the amount out to the last penny, opening a new account at another bank in the name of Borden Finchley, conservator."

Mason chuckled. "If the guy wants to get technical with me, I'll get technical with him."

"What will Judge Ballinger say about it?"

"I don't know," Mason said. "I think the judge is rather broadminded and I think he has a pretty shrewd suspicion there's something in this case that won't stand scrutiny. Of course, the fact that Daphne is no blood relative is the thing that puts us behind the eight ball. If it weren't for that, I'd walk into court and start shooting off fireworks. As it is now, I have no official standing the Court can recognize."

The telephone rang. Della Street picked up the instrument, said, "Yes, Gertie," and to Mason said, "that's probably Daphne calling now."

Mason nodded, started to reach for the telephone, then paused at the expression on Della's face.

She turned and said, "It's Dr. Alma and he says its very important that he talk to you immediately."

Mason nodded, picked up the phone, said, "Yes, Mason talking."

Dr. Alma's heavy masculine voice came over the wire.

"Mr. Mason," he said, "I'm down here at the so-called Goodwill Sanitarium and Rest Home. As you know, I came here under court order to examine Horace Shelby."

"What about him?" Mason asked. "Nothing's happened to him, has it?"

"A good deal has happened to him," Alma said.

"Good heavens, he isn't dead!"

"We don't know," Alma said. "He isn't here."

"He isn't there?"

"That's right."

"What happened? Did they let Finchley take him out somewhere?"

"I don't know and I'd like very much to find out," Dr. Alma said. "The man is gone. They say he's 'escaped.'

"Before anyone has a chance to clutter up the evidence any more, I'd like to find out. . . . You have a private detective who works with you, who has quite a bit of experience in investigation, I believe."

"That's right," Mason said.

"And you yourself are a legendary figure. I wonder if you and your detective could get out here?"

"Will they let us in?" Mason asked, winking at Della Street.

"Let you in?" Dr. Alma exploded. "*I'll* let you in! I'll turn this place wrong side out if they don't put all of their cards on the table and play ball right down the line!"

"I'll be right out," Mason said.

Mason slammed up the telephone receiver, grabbed his hat, said to Della Street, "Call Paul Drake. Tell him to take his car and join me at the Goodwill Sanitarium in El Mirar. Call Daphne Shelby again. Get her alerted to what has happened. Tell her to sit tight and wait for word from us—not to leave the hotel room."

"If she doesn't answer?" Della Street asked.

"Have her paged," Mason said. "I'm on my way."

The lawyer dashed out of the door and sprinted down the corridor.

It took Mason thirty-four minutes' fast driving to reach El Mirar.

He slammed his car to a stop at the parking place near the gate and noticed, without attaching any significance to the fact, that the signs asking for help had now been removed and that the door to the office was standing wide open. The woman who had been so curt the afternoon before was now effusive in her greeting.

"Doctor is expecting you, Mr. Mason. They're down in Unit 17. It's right down this walk to the right."

"Thank you," Mason said. "A private detective by the name of Paul Drake will be out here any minute. When he comes, send him down to Unit 17."

"Yes, indeed," she said, and her hard mouth twisted into what was intended as a cordial smile. Her eyes, however, were cold, blue and hostile.

Mason hurried down the walk to Unit 17, a small cottage standing in a row of similar cottages.

The lawyer heard angry voices from inside.

He walked up to the porch and jerked the door open.

The tall man who whirled to face the lawyer as he entered the room was somewhere in his forties—alert, slightly stooped, almost as tall as Mason, and, quite obviously, very indignant.

The other and older man was a head shorter — an apologetic, cowed individual who was very much on the defensive.

Mason sized up the situation at a glance.

"Dr. Alma?" the lawyer asked of the tall man.

Dr. Alma's indignant smoldering eyes focused on Perry Mason, then softened. "You're Perry Mason," he said.

"Right."

The two men shook hands.

"And this is 'Dr.' Tillman Baxter."

Mason didn't offer to shake hands with Dr. Baxter.

"*Dr.* Baxter," Dr. Alma went on, "is licensed as a naturopathic physician in another state. He has theories about diet."

"I'm licensed to run this rest home," Baxter said.

"Doubtless you are," Dr. Alma said, "but how much longer that condition is going to exist is anyone's guess. Now, I want to know everything there is to know about Horace Shelby. You say you don't keep charts."

"This isn't a regular hospital," Baxter protested. "This is a rest home."

"And you don't keep records of treatment?"

"We keep records of the important things."

"What do you consider important?"

"Anything which indicates a change in the physical or mental condition of the patient."

"You've told me you don't keep a record of drugs that are administered?"

"We do not administer drugs. That is, as a rule."

"What do you do?" Dr. Alma asked.

"We give our patients rest, privacy, and healthful food. We—"

"I was told that Horace Shelby was under heavy sedation," Mason said. "Who gave it to him?"

"Heavy sedation?" Dr. Baxter asked lamely.

"That was my understanding," Mason said.

"An outside private physician had been prescribing for Mr. Shelby," Dr. Baxter said. "We, of course, honor prescriptions given by the patient's own doctor."

"Who is this doctor?"

"I can't remember his name right now."

Mason looked around the room, taking mental inventory of an iron frame hospital bed, washstand, chest of drawers with a mirror, worn linoleum on the floor, drab lace curtains on the window.

"Where does this door go?" Mason asked.

"The bathroom," Dr. Baxter said.

Mason jerked the door open, looked at the old-fashioned bathtub, the toilet, the worn linoleum, the crowded cubicle, the wavy mirror over the shallow medicine cabinet.

"This other door?" the lawyer asked.

"The closet. That's where the patient keeps his clothes."

"I looked in there," Dr. Alma said. "The clothes are gone."

Mason looked in the closet at the row of clothes hooks along the wall.

"He took everything?" Mason asked.

"As nearly as we can tell, everything." Dr. Baxter said. "Of course, the man had virtually no personal possessions. An attendant shaved him. The man had a toothbrush and toothpaste and those are left in the medicine chest in the bathroom. Aside from that, he had virtually nothing except the clothes he wore when he was received."

"In other words," Mason said, "the man had no idea he was being taken to a sanitarium when he was railroaded in here."

"I didn't say that," Dr. Baxter said, "and I couldn't say it because frankly I don't know."

"A man going to a sanitarium carries at least a suitcase of clothes," Mason said. "Pajamas, underwear, shirts, socks, handkerchiefs."

"A *normal* man does," Dr. Baxter said.

"And Horace Shelby wasn't normal?"

"By no means. He was irritable, nervous, excited, aggressive and refused to co-operate."

"Who brought him here?"

"His relatives."

"How many?"

"Two of them."

"Borden Finchley and Ralph Exeter?"

"Finchley was one; I don't know the name of the other person. There was a nurse with them, too."

"Mrs. Finchley?"

"I believe so."

"And the three of them strong-armed Shelby into this room?"

"They registered him in the sanitarium. He was disturbed at the time, but the nurse gave him some sedation."

"You know what the sedation was?"

"It was a hypodermic."

"Did she tell you what it was?"

"She said it had been prescribed by his regular physician."

"Did you see a copy of the prescription? Did you know who the physician was?"

"I took her word for it. She was a registered nurse."

"In this state?"

"I believe in Nevada, I don't know."

"How do you know she was a registered nurse?"

"She told me so and, of course, from the way she handled the situation I could see that she had had training."

Mason suddenly backed into the room, picked up one of the straight-backed chairs, carried it into the closet, climbed up on it and reached back into the dark recesses of the closet shelf.

"What are these?" he asked, bringing out a set of straps.

Dr. Baxter hesitated, coughed, said, "Those are straps."

"Of course, they're straps," Mason said. "They're web straps. What's their purpose?"

"We use them to restrain patients who are inclined to become physically unmanageable—they use them in all hospitals which treat mental cases."

"In other words, you strap a man in bed?"

"When his condition requires."

"And Horace Shelby was strapped in bed?"

"I am not sure. He may have been at one time."

"And how long was he strapped in bed?"

"I would assume a very brief interval. We only use those straps when the patient becomes entirely unmanageable, and at times when we are somewhat shorthanded. You can see yourself that the straps have been removed, Mr. Mason."

"They've been removed, all right," Mason said, holding out two pieces of the strap. "They've been cut with a sharp knife."

"Dear me, so they have!" Dr. Baxter exclaimed.

"Then," Mason said, "if Horace Shelby escaped, as you claim, he must have had outside aid. Somebody must have cut those straps. A man who has been strapped in bed and has no knife can't very well cut the straps which are holding him."

Baxter said nothing.

Mason glanced at Dr. Alma.

Dr. Alma said, "I'm going to give this place a good airing. I'm going to find out what it's all about. Did you start this place, Baxter?"

"*Dr.* Baxter," Baxter said.

"Did you start it?" Alma said, raising his voice.

"No. I am buying it from the man who had started it."

"He's a licensed M.D.?"

"I didn't inquire paticularly into his qualifications. I saw the license to operate the place and I had that license assigned to me."

"By whom?"

"By the person who sold it to me."

"You'd better be in court at two o'clock this afternooon," Dr. Alma said. "I think Judge Ballinger is going to want to talk with you."

"I can't be in court. It's a physical impossibility. I have many patients and I am shorthanded. We have been doing everything in our power to attact competent help but we simply can't get them."

"Nurses?"

"We have practical nurses," Baxter said. "And we have one trained nurse, but much of our trouble is in getting competent household help. We are all of us doing double duty at the present time."

There were steps on the porch.

Paul Drake's voice said, "Hello, Perry."

"Come in," Mason said.

Drake entered the room. Mason said, "Dr. Grantland Alma, Mr. Drake; and *Dr.* Baxter."

"You're the detective?" Dr. Alma asked.

"Right," Mason said.

"I think Mr. Mason has uncovered the key clue," Dr. Alma said.

"Key clue?" Drake asked.

"To the disappearance of Horace Shelby."

"The escape of Horace Shelby," Dr. Baxter corrected.

"As far as I am concerned," Dr. Alma said, "the man is gone and I don't know how he went, where he went, or who took him."

"He took himself," Dr. Baxter said.

"You believe that?" Dr. Alma asked.

"Yes."

"All right," Dr. Alma said, "I'm going to quote you on that."

"What do you mean?"

"You've been holding him here as an aged incompetent," Dr. Alma snapped, "a man who was disoriented, who couldn't take care of himself, who was incapable of managing his affairs.

"When he resented that treatment, you strapped him down to the bed. You wouldn't allow visitors to see him. You wouldn't allow an attorney to consult with him.

"Now then, you adopt the position that this man was shrewd enough to find some way of cutting the straps that held him, getting up out of bed, dressing, getting out of the gate, out to the street—an aged, infirm man without enough money to get on a bus and, yet, he's vanished.

"Now then, you just come into court and say that you thought he was aged, infirm, senile, and unable to take care of himself, and let's see what the Court has to say."

"Well, now, wait a minute, wait a minute," Dr. Baxter said hastily. "Of course, he could have had help. What I meant to say was that he didn't have any help from this institution. In other words, we weren't trying to spirit him away so that the process of the court couldn't be used in his case."

"It isn't what you *meant* to say; it's what you did say." Dr. Alma said. "As far as I am concerned, I'm finished. I'm going back and make my report to the Court. . . . How about you, Mason?"

"I can't see where there's anything to be gained by staying here," Mason said, looking at the unhappy and frustrated Dr. Baxter. "Particularly, since we're all due in court this afternoon. . . . I take it Dr. Baxter has been subpoenaed?"

"If he isn't, he will be," Dr. Alma snapped. "I'll see to that."

"Now, just a minute, just a minute," Dr. Baxter said. "I can't be running around going to court. I am shorthanded as it is and—"

"I know," Dr. Alma said with mock sympathy. "I have the same thing happen from time to time myself. They subpoena me to come to court and I lose a day at the office. It's one of the duties of the *profession,* eh, *Doctor?*"

Mason moved to the door, led Drake to one side. "You have the car that has the telephone in it?" the lawyer asked.

Drake nodded.

"All right," Mason said, "put men on the job. I want everybody you can pick up put under twenty-four-hour surveillance."

"What do you mean 'everybody'?"

"Exeter, Finchley, Mrs. Finchley, Dr. Baxter here—and stick around and see if you can get any clue as to how Horace Shelby left here."

Drake nodded.

Mason said, "I have a hunch someone pulled a fast one. I noticed yesterday that there were two signs asking for help to run the place. Those signs have now been taken down. That means that someone applied for a job last night and got the job—probably a night job. See if you can find out anything about that person because that could well have been a plant—someone that Borden Finchley put in here to get Horace Shelby out of sight so that Dr. Alma couldn't examine him.

"If you can get a line on that person—in case some person was hired last night—spare no expense to get all the information possible."

Drake nodded. "Will do. It's going to cost money."

"Let it cost money," Mason said. "We're in a fight and we're going for the jugular."

Chapter NINE

Promptly at two o'clock, Judge Ballinger took his place on the bench.

"This is the time heretofore fixed for a continued hearing in the matter of a conservator for the estate of Horace Shelby.

"I see that Dr. Grantland Alma, the physician appointed by the Court to examine Horace Shelby, is in court. Dr. Alma is the Court's own witness, and the Court would like to have you come forward and be sworn, Doctor."

Darwin Melrose was on his feet.

"If the Court please," he said, "before Dr. Alma is examined, I would like to make a statement to the Court."

"What is it?" Judge Ballinger asked.

"Mr. Perry Mason, attorney for Daphne Shelby, has used a device to circumvent the Court's order appointing a conservator for the estate and preventing Horace Shelby from being imposed upon by shrewd and designing persons.

"He has so manipulated things that fifty thousand dollars of the money in the estate has been turned over to Daphne Shelby, no blood relative of Horace Shelby and the very person from whom Horace Shelby was supposed to be protected by Court order."

"How did he do that?" Judge Ballinger asked. "Didn't you serve a copy of the Court's order on the bank?"

"If the Court will remember," Melrose said, "I had special orders made for the bank—orders which turned every penny of the account in Shelby's name to Borden Finchley, as conservator."

"Didn't the bank do it?" Judge Ballinger asked.

"The bank did it."

"Then how did Mason get possession of fifty thousand dollars of that money?"

"Not of that money, but of other monies."

"Covered in the order?" Judge Ballinger asked.

"Well," Melrose said, and hesitated.

"Go on," Judge Ballinger snapped.

"They were not covered in that specific order—not by the letter of the order; they were, however, covered by the spirit of the order."

"Well, before we go into that, let's find out how incompetent Horace Shelby is," Judge Ballinger said. "I know how busy Dr. Alma is. I know that this is his busy time of the afternoon when he has an office full of patients and I would like to have him on the stand now, have him examined and cross-examined and then permit him to return to his office."

Judge Ballinger turned to Dr. Alma, leaving Darwin Melrose uncomfortably aware that the initiative had been taken from him.

"Did you see Horace Shelby, Doctor?" Judge Ballinger asked.

"I did not."

"Why not?"

"He was no longer at the so-called sanitarium and rest home."

"Where is he?"

"I don't know."

"How did this happen?"

"Again, I don't know. I have my own idea from certain things I discovered."

"What things?"

"This so-called sanitarium is nothing but a rest home. It is under the management of a man who uses the title of a doctor but is, in my opinion, completely inexperienced in psychiatric medicine.

"We found evidence that Horace Shelby had been strapped to a bed—perhaps ever since he had been placed in the institution. We found that the institution keeps no charts on patients, no hospital records. In my opinion, it is a very poor place to keep a person who is quite evidently being held against his will.

"I tried to find out whether Mr. Shelby had, in some way, made an escape by himself or whether he had been removed by people in the institution who wanted to keep me from examining him.

"In connection with my inquiries, I received a very remarkable statement from the man who manages the institution. He said that, in his opinion, Mr. Shelby had contrived to effect an unaided escape.

"I asked him if that meant that this man, who was claimed incompetent to handle his own affairs and who had to be strapped into a bed to restrain him, had sufficient intelligence and ingenuity to get hold of a knife to cut the straps, to dress, to make his escape unseen from the institution without sufficient funds to summon a taxicab or even to pay fare on a bus, and vanish so that he couldn't be found. I pointed out that there was no other construction which could be placed upon his statement."

"If the Court please," Darwin Melrose interposed, his face red, "I respectfully insist that this is not proper testimony from a psychiatrist, even if he has been appointed by the Court. He is giving conclusions, not from an examination of the patient but from surmises which he made as to the actual meaning of Dr. Baxter's statement that the patient had escaped."

Judge Ballinger frowned thoughtfully. "A very logical interpretation, certainly," he said. . . . "Does *anyone* know where Horace Shelby is at the present time? And I am asking this question particularly of counsel. I intend to hold counsel responsible for the actions of their clients in this matter."

Melrose said, "I want to assure the Court that I have no idea where Horace Shelby is, and my client, Borden Finchley, and his wife, Elinor Finchley, have assured me that they have no information; and Ralph Exeter, who has been visiting in the house with them, tells me that he has no information.

"I understand, however, that Daphne Shelby, the young woman who tried to establish relationship, is absent from her hotel; that messages have been unclaimed; and, despite the fact she knew that this hearing had been continued to this hour, she is not present. And I feel further that her counsel doesn't know where she is."

Judge Ballinger frowned. "Mr. Mason?" he asked.

Mason got to his feet slowly, turned as he heard the door open and said, without changing his expression by so much as the flicker of an eyelash, "Since Daphne Shelby has just walked into court, I suggest that she can speak for herself."

Daphne came rushing forward. "Oh, Mr. Mason, I am so sorry. I got caught in a traffic jam and—"

"That's all right," Mason said. "Just be seated."

Mason turned to the Court and said, "As far as I am concerned, Horace Shelby's disappearance came as a big surprise to me. I was summoned to the sanitarium by Dr. Alma and that was the first intimation I had that Mr. Shelby was no longer there."

Judge Ballinger said, "The Court isn't going to try a moot case. If it is impossible for Dr. Alma to examine Horace Shelby, the Court is going to continue the case until he can examine the man."

"But what about this manipulation of property so that fully fifty thousand dollars of the ward's estate has been spirited out from under control of the Court by Mr. Mason's subterfuge?"

Judge Ballinger looked at Mason, then at Melrose. There was a trace of a smile on his countenance. "Did Mr. Mason specifically violate any order of this Court?" he asked.

"No order that had been served on him—no, Your Honor."

"Did the bank violate any order of this Court?"

"Well . . . I believe the bank had notice that a conservator had been appointed."

"And the bank paid out funds which had been taken over by the conservator?"

"No, Your Honor. The bank paid out funds before the conservator had an opportunity to take them over."

"Didn't the order served on the bank specifically cover any and all accounts, credits, monies on deposit? And didn't the conservator order the account of Horace Shelby to be changed to the account of the conservator?"

"Not in exactly that way," Darwin Melrose said. "The order was that the bank pay over the entire sum that was in the account of Horace Shelby to the conservator."

"And where did this other money come from?"

"It was other monies that came in and were whisked out of the account before the conservator knew anything about them."

"But they were not specifically covered in the order served on the bank?"

"Not those funds, no."

Judge Ballinger shook his head. "The better practice would have been to have anticipated such a situation," he said. "We will take that up with the bank at a later date but certainly, as far as Mr. Mason is concerned, no order has been served on him. Mr. Mason's position is that the man was fully competent to carry on and transact his own business and, if this man had sufficient ingenuity to escape unaided from the institution where he was strapped to a bed, he would hardly seem to be disoriented, confused, senile and incompetent."

"We don't know that his escape was unaided," Darwin Melrose said.

"We certainly do not," Judge Ballinger pointed out, "and this is the thing which concerns the Court. It opens up rather sinister possibilities. If it should appear that Shelby was spirited out of that sanitarium so that Dr. Alma couldn't examine him, the Court is going to take very drastic steps.

"The matter will be continued until next Wednesday afternoon at four o'clock. In the meantime, court is adjourned."

Mason beckoned to Daphne to join him and once more led the way into the witness room.

"You've got to keep in touch with me, Daphne," he said sternly. "I've taken all sorts of chances on your behalf and I've been trying to get you. My office repeatedly has called, left messages at the hotel, and—"

"Oh, I'm sorry," she interrupted. "Mr. Mason, you'll have to forgive me just this once. I became involved in a matter and—I just can't explain now. I'd have been here in plenty of time if it hadn't been for that horrible traffic jam. Traffic on the freeway is getting so it's abslolutely impossible!"

"I know all about that," Mason said. "But I want you to keep in touch with my office. You have my telephone number; you can pick up the telephone and call me from time to time."

Her eyes refused to meet his. "Yes, I know," she said.

"Look here," Mason asked, "what have you been up to?"

Her eyes wide, innocent and naïve, raised to his. "What do you mean, what have I been up to?"

"I thought you were acting a little guilty," Mason said.

"Guilty of what?"

"I wouldn't know. You knew that your uncle has disappeared from the sanitarium?"

She said bitterly, "That's no surprise to me. They didn't dare to let a physician appointed by the Court examine him."

"That's the way it looks, all right," Mason said. "But sometimes the obvious deduction isn't the only deduction or the correct one.

"Now, I want you to keep in touch with my office, and I want you to keep in touch with your hotel so if I leave any messages for you, you can pick them up. Is that clear?"

"Yes. I'm very sorry, Mr. Mason."

"You said you'd been having trouble with traffic," Mason asked. "Were you riding with somebody?"

"No, oh no. I— Well, in a way. . . . I was using a friend's car."

"What friend?" Mason asked.

"Uncle Horace."

"His car?" Mason said. "Why, Finchley took over his car at the same time he took over the bank account and all that."

She lowered her eyes again and said, "This was one that Mr. Finchley didn't know about."

Mason said, "Look here, young lady, I've got to get back to my office. I have two or three lines out. I think you'd better come up there in about an hour and let's find out a little more about this."

"But what is there to find out?"

"I don't know," Mason said. "That's what I want to investigate. How did you get hold of another car belonging to Horace Shelby?"

"It was one he had."

"That they didn't know about?"

"Yes."

"A good car? Any good?" he asked.

"Practically new," she said.

Mason regarded her in frowning contemplation.

There was a knock on the door.

Mason opened it.

A court attaché said, "There's a telephone call for you, Mr. Mason. They say it's most important and that you're to take it right away."

"All right," Mason said. "Excuse me for a moment, Daphne."

Mason followed the attaché into the courtroom.

"You can take the phone on the clerk's desk," the officer said.

Mason nodded, picked up the telephone, said, "Hello," and heard Paul Drake's voice sharp with excitement.

"Did Daphne show up in court, Perry?"

"That's right."

"Tell you anything about where she had been?"

"No."

"Are you giving her a detailed examination as to where she's been and what she's been doing?"

"I've just started," Mason said.

"Forget it," Drake told him. "Let her go. Tell her to get in touch with you tomorrow morning. Let her go."

Mason said, "She's acting rather strangely, Paul, and she says there's another automobile that Finchley doesn't know about—"

"I'll say there is," Drake interrupted. "There's a lot no one knows about. Now, I haven't time to explain, but for heaven's sake let her go. Get her started. I want her on her way. I'll see you at your office shortly after you get there and explain."

"Wait a minute," Mason said. "I'm beginning to get the glimmer of an idea. You checked on the tip I gave you that some woman might have applied for a job and got a job at the sanitarium last night?"

"Right."

"Is there," Mason asked, looking over his shoulder to make certain that no one was listening, and lowering his voice, "any chance that—"

"Don't mention it over the phone," Drake said. "There's all the chance in the world. Meet me in your office and don't let Daphne know you're suspicious."

"Okay," Mason said. "I'll be there in twenty minutes."

The lawyer hung up the telephone and returned to the witness room.

There was no sign of Daphne.

Mason left the witness room, went to the outer office of Judge Ballinger's chambers and said to the judge's secretary, "Will you ask the judge if I can see him for a few moments on a matter of some importance?"

The secretary picked up the phone, relayed the message, said to Mason, "Judge Ballinger says for you to come on in."

Mason nodded, walked past the secretarial desk, and into the judge's private chambers.

"Judge," he said, "I made a statement in open court which was entirely true at the time I made it, but the situation has changed somewhat."

Judge Ballinger regarded him with not unfriendly eyes. "You understand, of course, Mr. Mason, that this is a bitterly contested matter and that I don't want you to say anything which would embarrass you or which might tend to disqualify me from hearing the case."

"I understand," Mason said. "This was in connection with a statement I made in open court, that I had no idea as to the whereabouts of Horace Shelby."

Judge Ballinger's eyes grew hard. "That statement was not correct?" he asked.

"That statement was entirely correct," Mason said.

"But since you have made it, you do know where Horace Shelby is?"

"No," Mason said, "but I think it is only fair to tell you that I have unearthed a clue which may lead me to Mr. Shelby before the hearing in this matter is resumed."

Judge Ballinger thought that over, then said, "I think it will be all right for you to tell me what the clue is because the Court is *most* anxious to have Dr. Alma get in touch with Shelby at the earliest possible moment. In fact, without committing myself in any way, I think I may say that it is quite important that the contact be made as soon as possible."

"I understand," Mason said. "I can, if you wish, tell you the clue."

"I think it will be all right for you to tell me that much," Judge Ballinger said.

Mason said, "There is a possibility that Daphne Shelby knows where her uncle is."

Judge Ballinger raised his eyebrows. Human curiosity struggled with judicial prudence, and human nature won out.

"What makes you think so?" Judge Ballinger asked.

"There is evidence," Mason said, "that Daphne Shelby purchased a car and took immediate delivery, that she may very well have gone to the Goodwill Sanitarium at El Mirar where she was not known and secured a position as a night nurse."

"That was last night?" Judge Ballinger asked.

"That was last night."

"Have you asked Daphne Shelby about this?"

"I haven't had an opportunity. I only learned it myself just a minute or two ago."

Abruptly Judge Ballinger threw his head back and laughed.

Mason stood silently waiting.

Judge Ballinger controlled himself, said, "Mason, I can't say anything without putting myself in a compromising position. However, if it's any satisfaction to you, this Court wasn't born yesterday.

"I'm glad you told me what you did because it puts my mind at ease about a matter which was causing me considerable concern. I think this conversation, however, has gone quite far enough and it is, of course, just between the two of us. I think it was your duty to tell me. I will also say this, that in the event you do have any personal contact with Horace Shelby, I want Dr. Alma to examine him at once. For reasons which I am not going to mention and which I don't think I need to go into at this time, I think it is highly important that the examination take place at the earliest possible moment."

Mason nodded. "I think I understand you."

"I'm quite certain you do," Judge Ballinger said, and then added, "and you yourself weren't born yesterday."

Chapter TEN

Paul Drake was waiting in Mason's office when the lawyer fitted his latchkey to the door of the private office and entered.

Mason glanced at Della Street. "Any calls, Della?"

She shook her head.

Mason turned to Drake. "What happened, Paul?"

"I can't tell you for sure," Drake said, "because I have been afraid to tip my hand by asking too many direct questions, but here's the story in a nutshell.

"Yesterday afternoon, a girl who answers the description of Daphne Shelby stopped a brand-new-looking car in front of the sanitarium and said she had noticed the sign that they wanted domestic help.

"It seems the sanitarium is pretty well filled and they were badly in need of help. They wanted someone to go to work making beds, sweeping, cleaning, and doing a general job of practical nursing.

"The girl who had been on the shift from ten o'clock at night until seven o'clock in the morning had quit, and our friend Dr. Baxter was desperate. This girl—I'm going to call her Daphne because I'm satisfied that's who she was—said she'd be back at ten o'clock to start work.

"No one got the license number on her car. She gave the name of Eva Jones, and said she'd had some nursing experience caring for aged people.

"Dr. Baxter didn't waste any time examining her credentials. He just needed someone in the worst way and he took her on.

"She worked during the entire night; was alert, intelligent, and on the job. Dr. Baxter got up and checked her a couple of times and everything seemed to be running fine.

"They had a cook and two more so-called nurses who came on duty at six o'clock in the morning to prepare breakfast; and then, after breakfast, to make beds.

"Those were experienced people who had been with the institution for some time and knew the ropes. The big trouble they had was keeping someone on night duty—the so-called 'graveyard shift' from ten until seven o'clock in the morning.

"This new girl was last seen about five-forty-five in the morning. When the cook came to the sanitarium, the new girl was there. She was supposed to stay until seven and help get the breakfast ready, but no one saw her after the cook greeted her.

"For a while, everyone was busy with breakfast and getting things started, and then they went into Unit 17 to make up the bed and see what could be done for the occupant who had been giving them a lot of trouble. They'd had to forcibly restrain him.

"They found the bed empty. Horace Shelby had vanished and the new girl had vanished.

"They didn't think too much about the significance of the girl not being on duty. Everyone thought she had misunderstood the hours she was to work, and they still feel that she'll be on duty tonight at ten.

"I followed up your lead about the 'Help Wanted' signs, found out Eva Jones had been employed, and pretended that I was a credit man trying to get a credit rating on Eva Jones, asked about what they knew about her background, got her residence address, and—most important of all—the physical description.

"I went to the residence address. It was phoney—a rooming house. They'd never heard of Eva Jones. What's more, they didn't have anyone who answered the physical description of Eva Jones living there.

"Now then, Perry, you can put two and two together. She bought a car; she went out and parked it at the sanitarium; she didn't duck out during the night because that would have been too much of a coincidence; she waited until the cook came on duty in the morning and then slipped in, cut the straps that were holding Horace Shelby to the bed, using a sharp butcher knife she had picked up from the kitchen. She got Shelby's clothes on him, got him across the yard, through the gate and into the automobile."

Mason nodded thoughtfully. "What about the car?"

"I've traced the records through the bank and the Motor Vehicle Department. Daphne Shelby bought a Ford automobile from a downtown agency yesterday and wanted immediate delivery. She paid for the car with a cashier's check drawn on the Investors National Bank and signed by the cashier.

"Because she was in such a hurry, the automobile agency people were a little suspicious, but they took the check to the bank and cashed it, rushed through the registration and delivered the car.

"The license is LJL 851—but, as I mentioned, no one got the license number of the car the so-called Eva Jones had when she drove up to the sanitarium. Apparently, it was a new Ford."

Mason, who had seated himself with one hip on a corner of his desk, one leg swinging back and forth, frowned thoughtfully.

"Our little naïve, unsophisticated girl seems to have a head on her shoulders and a lot of initiative."

"What's the Court going to say about all that?" Drake asked.

"That depends," Mason said thoughtfully.

"On what?" Della Street asked.

"On just what the facts are. If Horace Shelby is being railroaded into incompetency, that's one thing.

"On the other hand, *if* Borden Finchley was acting in good faith and believed that Daphne had been wheedling Horace and insinuating herself into his good graces so that she could make away with a large chunk of money, that's something else.

"Once Horace Shelby is interviewed by Dr. Alma, he'll tell the true story of how he was treated at the sanitarium, about being strapped to a bed, and all the rest of it.

"If the conspirators are railroading him, they can't afford to have *that* happen. They'll put a stop to it at all costs."

"What do you mean 'at all costs'?" Della Street asked.

"Murder," Mason said.

"Murder?" Della exclaimed.

Mason nodded.

"But how will murder help?" Della Street asked.

"Murder in itself won't help," Mason said. "They'll have to commit a murder that they can blame on Daphne Shelby. Their story will be very simple, that Daphne got Horace out of the sanitarium; that she got him to make a will leaving everything in her favor; that he died during the night. His death will seem to be from natural causes, but those causes were helped along by Daphne. We've got to find Daphne in order to protect her, from herself and from the others."

Drake said, "I've got men shadowing Daphne from the time she left the courthouse. We've got the license number of the automobile she's driving, and we should know where she's holed up within the next few minutes."

Mason looked at his watch. "She may have decided not to go directly to the hideout."

"What do we do when we get her located?" Drake asked.

"Notify Dr. Alma, take him out there and let him examine Horace."

"And if Shelby is confused and disoriented?"

"Then we'll put him in a good hospital under the care of Dr. Alma, go to court and see what we can do about getting another conservator appointed."

"And if he isn't confused?"

Mason grinned. "Then we accuse the Finchleys of criminal conspiracy, get them thoroughly discredited, get Horace Shelby declared competent and then—if he wants to, and apparently he does—let him make a will leaving all of the property to Daphne. And by that time, the show will be over."

"The Finchleys are gambling for high stakes," Drake said.

Mason nodded.

The unlisted telephone rang.

Della Street answered it, said, "It's for you, Paul."

Drake picked up the instrument, said, "Drake speaking. . . . Yes, hello, Jud— What? . . . How did that happen?"

Drake listened for a full minute, then said, "Where are you now? . . . Okay, wait there for instructions."

Drake hung up the telephone, turned to Mason and said, "I'm sorry, Perry, but they lost her."

"Lost her!" Perry Mason exclaimed.

"Well, they didn't lose her; she gave them the slip."

"How come?"

"I had to work fast," Drake said. "I had a man waiting at the courthouse to pick her up when she came out. There was a parking problem and she got a little head start. But I don't think that was what caused it. What really caused it was that she knew she was being tailed and was smart enough so she never let on."

"What makes you think that?"

"Because she took elaborate precautions to see that no one could follow her."

"What sort of precautions?"

"She was moving along with traffic, apparently entirely oblivious of her surroundings. She turned into a side street and suddenly whipped the car into a U-turn which was illegal, right in the middle of a busy boulevard—not a freeway, but a pretty important through boulevard.

"Of course, when you pull a maneuver like that you're able to pick the time and the place where you can make a quick U-turn without giving any signal. If an officer happens to pick you up, you're hooked. But if you get away with it, you're pretty apt to be in the clear because the maneuver takes the person who is following entirely by surprise. But if the boulevard is reasonably busy, by the time he gets his own car in a position where *he* can make a U-turn, it's too late.

"That's what happened in this case. Daphne made a U-turn right in front of a whole stream of cars that were bunched up because they'd been held up by a traffic signal a couple of blocks down the street. By the time my operative managed to make a U-turn, fifteen or twenty cars were between him and Daphne. And Daphne swung down a side street, went around the block, came to an intersection where she could have either gone straight ahead, to the right or the left. My man assumed she hadn't gone straight ahead because he couldn't see her. He had a choice of right or left. He chose right because usually a person trying to get away from someone will make a right-hand turn if it's clear.

"Well, it's the same old story. Once you've lost a person you're very lucky if you get them back in your sights. He came to another intersection, had the same choice to make, and somewhere along the road he made the wrong choice."

"Now," Mason said, "Daphne has really got herself in a jam. If she isn't on the square, the Court is going to feel that she is deliberately interfering with the process of the Court; and if she is acting in good faith and Borden Finchley can find her before we do, she's in danger and Horace is in danger."

"You really think they'd resort to murder?" Della Street asked.

"I don't know," Mason said. "All I know is it's a big possibility in the case, and it's up to a lawyer to look at possibilities.

"Paul, round up every man you can get on short notice. Put them on the freeway leading into El Mirar. Watch for Daphne Shelby's car."

"She wouldn't be in El Mirar," Paul Drake said. "She wouldn't dare."

"I think that's the only place she does dare to be," Mason said.

"Put yourself in her position. She went out to the sanitarium at El Mirar to see if she could get a job. In the event she could get a job, she intended to make an escape with Horace Shelby, and she was smart enough to figure out the details of that escape so she could pull it at a time when it wouldn't attract too much attention.

"On the other hand, she couldn't be certain that someone wouldn't see them leaving the place or that, through some circumstance she hadn't anticipated, the escape would be discovered before they had been gone very long.

"Therefore, the smart thing for her to have done was to have driven out to El Mirar in the afternoon, gone to some motel, explained that she wanted twin units, that her uncle was going to join her later.

"Then, when she had the stage all set, she simply showed up with the uncle.

"I was interested in the statement she made to me about being late for court. She said that traffic on the freeway was terrible and it had taken her longer than she had anticipated.

"At the time, I didn't know she was driving a car and I wondered just what she meant.

"I think it was a case of blurting out the simple truth before she realized what a statement of that sort would mean."

Drake nodded. "Okay, Perry," he said. "Let me go down to my place. I can get better action on the men I want to put out down there."

Mason said, "Cover the motels at El Mirar. See if you can't find Daphne Shelby's new car parked in front of one of the units."

Chapter ELEVEN

It was just as Perry Mason and Della Street were closing the office that Paul Drake's code knock sounded on the door.

Della opened the door and Mason said, "Hi, Paul, we've been waiting to hear from you but had decided to go out and have a cocktail and a little dinner—thought we'd drop by your office and give you an invitation. Since you're here, we'll give you the invitation in person."

Drake grinned. "You're dangling temptation in front of my nose," he said, "but I'll proably be sending out for hamburger sandwiches and drinking coffee out of a paper cup."

"What gives?" Mason asked. "Have you struck pay dirt?"

"We've not only struck pay dirt, we've got Daphne Shelby."

"The deuce," Mason said. "Where?"

"Your hunch paid off," Drake told him. "I started men looking for automobiles parked in motels around El Mirar, and we finally located the car at the Serene Slumber Motel. She's in Unit 12 and she's all alone."

"Alone?" Mason asked.

Drake nodded.

Mason walked back to the desk, sat down in the big swivel chair and started drumming softly on the edge of the desk with the tips of his fingers.

"And what has happened to Horace Shelby?" Della Street asked.

Mason said, "She may have him hidden out. He's probably in another unit and—"

"Not in the Serene Slumber," Drake interrupted. "My men are thorough enough for that. They checked every unit and quizzed the people who are running the place. There's no single, unattached elderly man in the place, and Daphne Shelby has just the one unit and she's alone in there."

"What name is she registered under?" Mason asked.

Drake grinned. "Her own name."

"Thank heavens for that," Mason said. "It will give us something to work on when they catch her."

"They'll catch her?" Drake asked.

"Probably," Mason said. "But the person we're interested in right at the moment is Horace Shelby. They'll certainly be trying to corral him, and if the Finchley crowd gets him before Dr. Alma can have a chance to examine him, you can't tell what's going to happen.

"I'll tell you what you do, Paul, keep a tail on Daphne and let's see if she isn't keeping him hidden in some other motel."

"What would be the object of that?" Drake asked.

"Darned if I know," Mason said, "but I have a hunch she's trying to cover her trail so that if anyone locates her they can't automatically put their hands on Horace Shelby.

"Come on, Paul, put your men out on the job and leave word where you can be reached. Have a cocktail and then a nice thick steak, a baked potato filled with butter, some French fried onion rings and—"

"Don't, you're killing me," Drake said.

"Those hamburgers will be soggy by the time you get them sent up to the office," Della Street said. "The coffee will taste of the paper cup, and—"

"Sold!" Drake exclaimed.

"Come on," Mason told him. "We'll stop by your office and leave word where they can catch you on the telephone."

Drake said, "Something seems to tell me the case is going to get hot all at once and I *should* be where I can get on the phone and put out men."

"We'll go someplace reasonably close," Mason promised.

"I've already succumbed to the temptation," Drake told him, "so you can ease off on the sales talk. Let's go."

They stopped by Drake's office on their way to the elevator. Drake left minute instructions with the switchboard operator in charge, said to Mason, "All right, let's hurry. I'll bet you that I get my appetite sharpened with a cocktail, that we order our steaks and just as they are put on the table the phone will ring with an emergency that will send me scampering and I'll wind up with—"

"A steak sandwich," Della Street said. "We'll get the waiter to bring you a bowser bag as soon as you order and you can have some French bread all buttered and waiting."

"You may think you're kidding," Drake said, "but as a matter of fact, that's exactly what I'm going to do. You've got an idea."

They went to the Purple Lion Restaurant which was one of Mason's favorites and was within easy cab distance of the office.

They had a cocktail and ordered their dinners at the same time they ordered the cocktail.

"Now then," Mason told the waitress, "bring a bowser bag, bring the freshest sourdough French bread you have in the place, and lots and lots of butter, both for the baked potato and for the steak sandwich."

"Steak sandwich?" the waitress said. "Why, I have orders for three extra thick steaks, but—"

"This man may have to make his into a steak sandwich and leave in a rush," Mason told her.

"Oh, I see," she said, smiling. "All right, we'll have the cocktails immediately. I'll have the steaks put on the fire and the bread and the bowser bag will come while you're drinking the cocktails."

Drake grinned and said, "Not a bad idea. If necessary I could eat a steak sandwich in the taxicab on my way to the office— What the deuce do you suppose she's doing sitting out there all by herself?"

"She's awaiting developments of some sort," Mason said. "But you can gamble on one thing—she isn't going to let Horace Shelby go wandering around unchaperoned, even if he's in a fit condition to do so."

"So?" Drake asked.

"So," Mason said, "somewhere along she's going to see that he has dinner. After all, the guy has to eat, you know."

"Well, let's hope she didn't give him a hamburger," Drake said. "Those things are fine when you eat them while they're fresh, but when you put them in a paper bag the bread gets soggy and— Oh, I guess they're all right, but I've eaten so darned many of them sitting up there in the office with a telephone at my ear that I just don't like the idea."

"Why don't you get something else?" Mason asked.

"What else can you have sent in?" Drake asked. "What takes place of a good old hamburger sandwich with lots of onions?"

"Well, when you put it that way," Mason said, "you make it sound appetizing."

The waitress brought their cocktails and the French bread, butter and the bowser bag for Paul Drake.

Drake made a ceremony out of buttering two thick slices of French bread.

They finished the cocktails and after a few minutes the waitress brought the steaks.

Della Street waived her feminine prerogative; pointing at Paul Drake she said, "Serve him first. He's apt to be called out."

The headwaiter approached the table. "One of you is Mr. Paul Drake?" he asked. "I have a call for you. Shall I plug the phone in here?"

Paul Drake groaned.

Mason nodded. "Bring the phone," he said.

Drake picked the steak off the plate with a fork, put it between the two slices of French bread.

As the waiter brought the telephone, Drake sliced a piece off the steak, started chewing on it; then, still chewing, picked up the telephone, said, "Yes, this is Drake."

The receiver made noises. Drake listened for a while, said, "Just a moment."

He turned to Mason, said, "The tail is reporting on Daphne Shelby. She went to a Chinese restaurant and ordered food to take out—chow mein, fried rice, barbecued pork and chicken pineapple. I'll get back to the office and—"

"Stay right here," Mason interrupted. "You won't have time to get to the office. What's she doing now?"

"She's waiting for the food. My man slipped to a telephone."

"She doesn't know she's being tailed?"

"No, apparently not. She looked around a bit when she started out, but apparently she feels pretty safe."

"Tell your man to keep on her tail," Mason said. "Don't take any chances of losing her. We've got to know where she goes. She's taking food to Horace Shelby right now."

"You mean I eat?" Drake asked with mock incredulity.

"You eat," Mason said. "Tell your man not to lose her under any circumstances."

Drake gave instructions in the telephone, slipped the thick steak out from under the pieces of buttered French bread, noted especially the stained surfaces of the bread where the steak juices had soaked in mingling with the melted butter.

He heaved an ecstatic sigh and said, "Sometimes, Perry, I think you're a slave driver, but this time I'm for you a million per cent. I thought you'd want to have me get Horace Shelby located, bolt my food and get out there."

Mason shook his head. "I want to find out what Daphne Shelby is up to first, Paul. There's something cooking and I don't know what it is."

"You don't think there's any chance the guy really is off his rocker and Daphne is keeping him stashed away?"

"I doubt it," Mason said. "If he were confused and disoriented, she wouldn't want to leave him alone and—After all, Paul, the guy's only seventy-five and the way we're living nowadays with vitamins and people being conscious of diet and cholesterol, a guy at seventy-five is just coming into the prime of life."

"Some of them get a little woozy at that age," Drake pointed out. "You know you have the testimony of the doctor who said he found him disoriented and confused."

"And, by the same token," Mason said, "we don't know what medication he had had before the doctor saw him."

The headwaiter took away the telephone. Drake attacked his steak, wolfing it down with swallows of hot coffee between bites.

Mason and Della Street ate more leisurely but without wasting time.

The waitress, sensing the urgency of the situation, hovered over the table.

Paul Drake dug out the last of the baked potato, rich with golden butter and red paprika on the top.

"That's the first time I've really enjoyed an evening meal in a long time. You'd be surprised how exacting this job is, Perry. And when *you* get a case, everything seems to go bang all at once."

"I'll admit I want lots of fast service," Mason said. "Somehow my cases seem to develop at high speed."

Drake said, "You're the high-speed factor. Once you start on something you whip it through to a conclusion. The other attorneys I work for keep office hours, go home at four-thirty or five o'clock, forget about business until eight-thirty or nine-thirty the next morning."

"They don't have my type of work," Mason said.

"No one does," Drake told him, grinning.

The headwaiter was apologetic as he returned with the phone the second time.

"For you, Mr. Drake," he said.

Drake grinned affably. "It's all right now," he said, "I've had my dinner. No hamburger tonight."

Drake picked up the telephone, said, "Drake speaking . . . Go ahead, Jim, what do you know?"

Drake was silent for a moment, then cupped his hand over the mouthpiece and said to Mason, "She took the food to the Northern Lights Motel, parked the car directly in front of Unit 21, gave a perfunctory knock on the door, then opened the door which was unlocked and went in with the food in two big bags."

"Then what?"

"Closed the door. She's there now. There's a phone booth at the corner and my man is in the phone booth."

"Tell him to keep an eye on the situation," Mason said, "and particularly notice the time element. I want to know what time she went in; I want to know what time she comes out; and I want to know where she goes when she leaves there. . . . How about some more coffee, Paul?"

"Are you kidding?"

"No, I'm serious."

Drake relayed Mason's instructions into the telephone, settled back in his chair with a grin. "Paul Drake," he announced to no one in particular, "is dining high on the hog tonight. I think I'll have a hot fudge sundae as well."

"May as well have whatever *you* want," Mason said. "I have an idea Daphne is going to be in there for some time and we have to wait here."

They had a leisurely dessert.

"Now what?" Drake asked when they had finished.

"We still wait," Mason said.

"We can go to my office," Drake suggested. "My men all call the office, and the office relays the call to wherever I happen to be."

Mason nodded. "Call your office. Tell them we're on our way back," he said.

"I hope you know what this is all about," Drake said. "It's all mixed up as far as I'm concerned."

"It's mixed up as far as *I'm* concerned," Mason admitted. "But I want to get a few high cards in my hand before I start calling for a showdown."

"You're calling for a showdown?" Drake asked.

"I'm going to have to," Mason said, "somewhere along the line."

"Tonight?"

Mason nodded, summoned the waiter, signed the check, gave the waitress an extra ten-dollar tip and said, "I just want you to know how much we appreciate the friendly service that you gave us."

Her face lit with pleasure. "Why—thank you *so* much. You're *so* nice!"

Mason detoured past the headwaiter, handed him another bill, said, "Thanks ever so much for keeping an eye on us, and, incidentally, the waitress who handled our table did a wonderful job, the sort of job that makes people want to come back."

The headwaiter bowed. "She's one of our best. I assigned her to your table, Mr. Mason."

"Thanks," Mason said.

Driving back to the office, Drake said, "Why all the flowery talk, Perry? The money would have been enough. That's what they care about."

Mason shook his head. "They like appreciation."

"You show it with money."

"No you don't," Mason said. "It takes both money and words. Money without words is vulgar. Words without money are cheap."

"I never thought of it exactly that way," Drake said. "But perhaps that's why you always get such good service in restaurants."

"Don't you?" Mason asked.

Drake grinned. "Sure, I send my secretary down to the restaurant for a couple of hamburgers with mustard and onion, and a pint of coffee. She always smiles when she brings it in. That's what you call service with a smile."

"We're going to have to do something about your eating," Mason said.

"You can say that again," Drake told him. "Now that I've found out how the other half lives, I'm ruined."

They dropped Paul Drake at his office. Mason and Della Street went on down to the lawyer's office.

"She's having dinner with Horace Shelby?" Della asked.

Mason nodded.

"And you're worried about the case, aren't you?"

Again Mason nodded.

"Why?"

"In the first place," Mason said, "my client has started taking shortcuts. I don't like that. In the second place, she isn't confiding in me and I don't like that. In the third place, the fact that she's taking such elaborate precautions to keep Horace Shelby out of circulation either means that he's pretty far out in left field or that both of them are afraid the Finchleys are going to put him back in that sanitarium and restrain him by force."

"Well," Della said, "after a man has been strapped to a bed; after he's been taken against his will and thrown into what is virtually a mental institution and all of that, he's going to dread any possibility of returning."

"That probably accounts for it," Mason said, "but the situation may be a lot more complicated than appears on the surface. . . . What do you suppose Borden Finchley and his wife are doing? What do you suppose Ralph Exeter is doing?"

"Doesn't Drake have men on them?"

Mason shook his head. "After his men picked up Daphne Shelby, I concentrated on her. The others are relatively unimportant, and I don't want Finchley reporting to the court that I had him shadowed."

"Do you think he'd know that he was being shadowed?" Della Street asked.

"He's pretty apt to find it out. A skillful shadow can tail a person for a while, but when you have three people to shadow, someone's going to get wise. And then, of course, if that one communicates his thoughts to the others and they begin to look around, it isn't too difficult to spot a shadow.

"Of course, it *can* be handled if you have the money to spend. You can alternate shadows, you can put several shadows on one suspect; you can have them behind him, ahead of him, and generally do a pretty good job. But I didn't want to take chances in this case, and therefore once we've found Horace Shelby that's what we're playing for. When we get him, we've hit the jackpot."

"And what are you going to do then?"

"It depends on the condition he's in," Mason said. "I'm going to play fair. As soon as we're dead certain we have him located, I'm going to get in touch with Dr. Alma and arrange for an interview. If Shelby is okay, I'm going to see what we can do for Daphne. If he isn't—if he's really in need of having someone look after him, then, of course, we're in a different situation.

"However, I am going to try and get evidence that will make the Court change its order in regard to Borden Finchley. I think we'll have some other conservator."

Mason walked around the office aimlessly, working off his restlessness while he was waiting.

Della, knowing that Perry Mason did much of his intensive thinking while pacing the floor, settled herself in the big, overstuffed leather chair, remaining motionless so as not to disturb the lawyer's thoughts.

The silence of night settled upon the big office building.

The sound of the unlisted telephone ringing shattered the silence.

Only three people had the number of that unlisted telephone— Perry Mason, Della Street and Paul Drake—so Mason scooped up the instrument and said sharply, "Yes, Paul."

Drake said, "My man just telephoned. She's back at the Serene Slumber Motel. He didn't have a chance to telephone when she came out of the Northern Lights. She just jumped in her car and started moving and he had to follow. He's at a phone now, waiting instructions."

"Tell him to wait until we get there," Mason said. "Unless, of course, she goes out. If she does, he's to follow her and report at the earliest opportunity. We can't afford to lose her now."

"Your car or mine?" Drake asked.

"Both," Mason said. "We may want to separate later. You take

your car and lead the way. Della will go with me. We'll pick you up
at your office and start out at once."

Mason hung up the telephone, nodded at Della Street, who already
had her hand on the light switch.

They hurried down the corridor, stopped at the illuminated ob-
long of Paul Drake's door. Mason was reaching for the doorknob
just as the door was opened from the inside and Drake emerged.

"All ready?" Drake asked.

"All ready," Mason said. "Let's go."

They rode down in the elevator, crossed to the parking lot, got in
their respective cars, and Drake led the way out to the freeway, then
along to the turnoff at El Mirar.

The lawyer knew that Drake had the telephone in his automobile
and saw the detective using it once in a while, apparently getting
directions as to the best way to get to the Serene Slumber Motel.

Drake drove unerringly, making good time, then blinked his brake
lights a couple of times to call Mason's attention to the illuminated
sign ahead which read, "Serene Slumber Motel" and, down near the
street, a red illuminated sign reading, *Sorry. No Vacancies.*

Drake pulled his car into the parking lot and usurped a vacant
place. It took Mason a few seconds to find a place where he could
leave his car. Since the marked parking stalls were all filled, it was
necessary for the lawyer to leave his car down at the curb at the far
end of the lot.

Mason and Della walked to join Paul Drake, who, by that time,
was standing close to the shadowy figure of a tall, young man.

"I think you know Jim Inskip," Drake said, by way of introduc-
tion; and then added, "This is Della Street, Mr. Mason's secretary."

Inskip bowed. "I've met you before, Mr. Mason, and I'm very
glad to meet you, Miss Street. Our party's in Unit 12."

"Any sign of leaving or turning in for the night?"

"Neither. Her car's here. You can see the lights on in the unit—
that's the one with the light right over there."

The detective pointed.

"What do we do, Perry?" Drake asked.

Mason said, "Inskip stays here and keeps the place covered. He is
to stay with Daphne Shelby no matter what happens. If we come out
and drive away, Inskip is not to come anywhere near us but is to sit
in his car and wait, because Daphne might be smart enough to turn

out the light and look out of the back window. We'll arrange our communication system by phone later on."

"You want me to come with you?" Drake asked.

"I think I do," Mason said, "but I may have to ask you to leave. Anything that a client says to a lawyer is a privileged, confidential communication; anything that a lawyer says to a client is a privileged, confidential communication.

"That privilege also applies to a lawyer's secretary, but if the lawyer takes along someone else as an audience, that person can be called to the stand to relate any conversation which took place. I may want to have certain parts of the interview confidential. A great deal will depend on just what she's trying to do and just what she hopes to accomplish."

The three of them separated from Inskip, moved around to the walk which went around the front of the units, and Mason tapped gently at the door of number 12.

There was no answer from within, although a faint illumination shone through the curtains.

Mason tapped again.

Again, there was no answer.

The third time, the lawyer's knock was loud and peremptory.

After a moment, the knob turned, the door opened a crack and Daphne Shelby said, "Who . . . who is it? . . . What do you want?"

Mason said, "Good evening, Daphne."

Daphne, light-dazzled eyes failing to penetrate the semidarkness, flung herself against the door, trying to close it, but Drake and Mason pushed their weight against the door and Daphne slid back along the carpet.

Mason held the door open while Della Street entered.

Daphne, apparently recognizing him for the first time, was wide-eyed with surprise.

"*You!*" she exclaimed. "How in the world did *you* get here?"

Mason said, "Daphne, I want to ask you some questions. I want you to be very careful how you answer them. Anything that you say to *me* is a privileged communication as long as only you, Della and I are in the room. But with Paul Drake, a detective, present, the communication is no longer privileged. Drake can be called as a witness. Now, if there are any questions I ask which are going to embarrass you, or anything you want to tell me which you don't want known, just speak up and Paul Drake will either step outside or step into the bathroom. Is that clear?"

She nodded wordlessly.

"All right," Mason said, "just what do you think you're accomplishing?"

"I'm trying to save Uncle Horace's sanity," she said. "He would have gone stark, staring, raving mad if I hadn't got him out of that place. Or did you know that I had got him out of the place?"

"I knew," Mason said. "Why didn't you tell me what you were intending to do?"

"I didn't dare. I was afraid you would stop me."

"Why?"

"Your ideas of professional ethics."

Mason regarded her thoughtfully.

She said after a moment, "I presume you know all that I've done."

Mason said, "You went out to the sanitarium. You saw from the sign that they were very anxious to get someone to do domestic work. You applied for the job."

She nodded.

"You bought a new car."

Again she nodded.

"All right," Mason said, "You went out and went to work. What happened?"

She said, "I'll never forget what I saw when I got out there. I started work. It took me a couple of hours before I dared to slip into Unit 17 where they were keeping Uncle Horace.

"There was that poor man strapped to a bed—absolutely strapped —and the straps were stretched so tight that they were holding him motionless."

"What was his mental condition?"

"What would your mental condition be in a situation like that? Here the poor man had been taken away from his home, had been stripped of his property. And they intended to leave him there until he died, and to do everything they could to hasten his death.

"Uncle Horace has always had claustrophobia—a fear of being rendered helpless where he couldn't move. And he was tied down there, he was moving his head and trying to get at his straps so he could bite them. He was wild and disheveled and—"

"Did he recognize you?" Mason asked.

She hesitated a moment and then said, "I don't think I'd better talk any more about that phase of it until you and I can be alone, Mr. Mason."

"All right," Mason said. "What else can we talk about now?"

"Well," she said, "I went back in the morning after the night's work had all been done and just before the morning shift came on— right after the cook came in. I had picked up a very sharp butcher knife in the kitchen and I cut through those straps. I found Uncle Horace's clothes in the closet and I got some clothes on him and got him out into the automobile and drove away."

"Did you think they would follow you?"

"Yes."

"Why didn't you keep Uncle Horace here with you?"

"I thought it would be safer to park him off by himself."

"Did he recognize you in the morning when you took him out?"

"Oh heavens, yes," she said.

"What's his mental condition now?"

"Pretty nearly normal, except when you mention something about the sanitarium he just goes all to pieces. He's on the verge of a complete nervous breakdown because of the things he's had to put up with."

"You knew they'd find out about what you did?" Mason asked.

"I felt they probably would, yes."

"You knew that they'd come looking for you?"

"That's why I got Uncle Horace where no one could ever find him."

Mason raised his eyebrows.

"No one will find him where he is," she said. "He's going to stay there until he's got his nerves back in shape and until we can get Finchley shown up for the type of man he is.

"Uncle Horace tells me that no sooner had I left for the Orient than they started doing all sorts of little things that they knew would irritate and annoy him. They treated him like a child. They wouldn't let him do what he wanted to. They started making him nervous. He thinks Aunt Elinor was giving him some drug that over-stimulated him. He couldn't sleep, and when he told her he couldn't sleep, she said she'd give him some sleeping pills.

"Within a week or ten days, he was so dependent on those sleeping pills that he had to have them in order to get a night's sleep. Otherwise he'd lie there and toss and get nervous, sleep for an hour or two, then lie awake for the rest of the night."

"Didn't it occur to him that Mrs. Finchley was deliberately drugging him?"

"Not at the time. She handed him a great line of talk about how he was upset because he was accustomed to having me around, but that the trip was the best thing on earth for me and that I was going to crack up if I didn't have some recreation and some help. And she pointed out to him that he was pretty much of a nuisance and needed altogether too much attention for one person to give it to him. And then she kept giving him more and more medication.

"Finally, he realized what they were trying to do. That was when he wrote that letter to me."

"Just what was his idea in writing that letter?"

"He wanted me to get enough money out of the bank account so that if they did start proceedings for a guardianship, he wouldn't be absolutely helpless."

"He realized what they had in mind?"

"By that time, yes; it was very obvious. . . . That's a horrible thing, Mr. Mason. They suddenly drag a man into court and claim that he's incompetent to manage his affairs and strip him of every cent he has in the world.

"How would you feel if you'd saved up enough money to be independent, and then relatives suddenly moved in and took all that money away from you and put you in some kind of an institution where—"

"I'd feel pretty bad," Mason said, "but that's not the point. Just what are your plans now?"

"I was intending to get in touch with you."

"You took long enough doing it."

"Well, I had to make arrangements to see that Uncle Horace would be safe and comfortable."

"Where is he?" Mason asked.

She clamped her lips together and shook her head.

Mason smiled. "You're not telling me?"

"No. I'm not going to tell a soul. Thay's why I have him where people can't get at him until he's ready to step into court and go in there fighting. And this time, he's not going to be drugged."

"He was drugged when he went to court?" Mason asked.

"Of course," she said scornfully. "You don't think that they could ever have pulled a fast one like that unless they had him drugged in such a way that he didn't have his normal responses."

"The judge didn't detect that he was drugged and the doctor that examined him didn't."

"They were rather clever but they had been brainwashing him for three months. Don't ever forget that! And with a man of that age, a very clever person can do a lot of brainwashing in three months."

"How is he now?" Mason asked.

She hesitated for a long moment, then said, "Better."

"And you gave him money?" Mason asked.

"I gave him forty thousand dollars of his money."

"Forty thousand dollars?" Mason asked.

She nodded. "I bought the car, and I'm keeping enough money so I can do the things that have to be done. I gave him the rest."

"Did you," Mason asked, "tell him about the evidence that had been brought out in court, that you weren't actually related to him?"

She said, "I don't think I want to talk about that for a while, but I can tell you this, he's made his will now."

Mason's eyes narrowed. "I was afraid of that," he said. "I wish you'd got in touch with me. That was the one thing he should never have done."

"Why?"

"Don't you see," Mason said, "you're playing right into their hands. They claimed that if you could ever get him where he was under your control, you'd have him make a will and you'd get his property.

"That letter he wrote with the check for a hundred and twenty-five thousand dollars was just the sort of thing they needed; and, if they can show that you had him make a will in your favor as soon as you got him out of the sanitarium, that also will be ammunition they can use."

"But this was his own idea," she said. "He wanted to do it. He insisted on it. He'd been trying to make a will so there couldn't be any question."

"Then he should have done it through an attorney and in the regular way," Mason said. "The document should have been formally witnessed. . . . What kind of a will did he make?"

"He said that in this state a will is good if it's entirely written, dated and signed in the handwriting of the testator; and you had told me the same thing, so that's the sort of will he made."

"Who has it?" Mason asked.

"I do."

"Give it to me."

She hesitated a moment, then opened her purse, took out a folded document and handed it to Mason.

Mason read the will. "This is all in his handwriting?"

"Yes."

Mason checked the points: Dated . . . Signed . . . Purporting to be a last will and testament . . . "You'd better let me keep this, Daphne."

"I want you to."

"And," Mason said, "say nothing about it unless you're asked. I want to get hold of Horace Shelby; and in the event he's competent, I want him to make a will setting forth whatever he wants to put in it, and I want to make certain it will be a valid will.

"Now then, let's go and see Horace Shelby."

She shook her head. "I am not going to tell you where he is."

"Suppose," Mason said, "that you just take a little ride with me and we'll go to see him."

She smiled. "And you can't bluff me, Mr. Mason. I know you regard me as a naïve child but I'm not as green as some people think."

"I'll say you're not," Mason said. He nodded significantly to Della Street and gestured toward the telephone directory.

Della moved quietly behind Daphne's chair to consult the directory and then, when she had the address she wanted, made a surreptitious note and nodded to Mason.

Daphne Shelby, in the meantime, had been glaring at Mason defiantly.

"I'm not going to tell you," she said. "And you're not going to bluff me by making me think you know so that I'll say something that will be a giveaway. I know all about that technique of getting information."

Mason smiled. "I'm sure you do," he said. "Well, get your hat and coat and we'll take a little ride."

"I'll ride with you," she said, "but I'm not going to give you any information about where Uncle Horace is. He needs rest; he needs to have the assurance that he's his own man once more. You just can't imagine what a devastating experience this has been for him."

"You gave him forty thousand dollars?" Mason asked.

"Yes."

"How?"

"I endorsed seven cashier's checks for five thousand dollars over to him and I gave him five thousand dollars in cash."

"A man in his condition shouldn't be carrying that money around with him," Mason said. "In fact, nobody should carry that much, but particularly your Uncle Horace shouldn't have it."

"It's his money!" she blazed. "And that's the only way he's ever going to snap out of it—is to feel that he's his own master, that he can do what he wants to with his own money."

"All right," Mason said, "let's get in the car. Perhaps you'd better follow us in your car, Paul."

"Will do," Paul Drake said.

"Perhaps you'd be so good as to tell me where you're taking me?" Daphne asked.

Mason grinned. "Just down the road a piece. We'll bring you back in due course. There's a man down there I want to see."

Her head held high, she stalked out to Mason's car.

Mason, Della Street and Daphne got into the front seat. With Paul Drake following, they drove down the thoroughfare, turned to the right, cruised past the Northern Lights Motel. Mason frequently glanced at Daphne's face.

The young woman kept looking straight ahead, not even her eyes turned as they cruised slowly past the motel.

Paul Drake, in the car behind Mason, snapped his lights on and off, gave two quick taps on the horn button.

Mason swung to the curb, rolled down the window on his side and waited.

Drake's car pulled alongside.

"What is it?" Mason asked.

"Cops," Drake said tersely.

"Where?"

"Other end of the motel. Two cars."

"Oh-oh," Mason said.

"What do we do?" Drake asked.

Mason said, "We pull around the corner and wait. You go ask questions. Not pointed questions but adroit questions."

"Will do," Drake said.

As the detective pulled away, Mason turned to Daphne and said, "That's what comes of trying to give your own attorney a double cross and taking things into your own hands.

"Now you can see what's happened. Finchley has found out where your Uncle Horace is. He's charged him with escaping from a sanitarium where he was confined under a Court order and has probably brought in police to take him back."

Daphne, who had been bravely silent, suddenly started to cry. "If they take him back to that sanitarium and strap him in bed, it will kill him," she said.

"We'll *try* not to let it happen," Mason told her. "We'll get out of the way and park and and see what we can do."

The lawyer eased the car into motion, came to the cross street and started to turn. A police car, with siren moaning a low but peremptory message for the right-of-way, came around the corner. Mason pulled to the curb.

The police car, traveling at slow speed, started past the lawyer's car, then suddenly stopped. The beam of a red spotlight illuminated the interior of Mason's car.

"Well, well, well," Lieutenant Tragg's voice said. "Look who's here!"

"Why, hello, Lieutenant," Mason said. "What are *you* doing here?"

"I think I'll ask you first and make the question official," Tragg said. "What are you doing here?"

"I had been out to see a client on a probate matter," Mason said, "and—"

"Your client live at the Northern Lights Motel?" Tragg interrupted.

Mason grinned and shook his head. "Why?"

"We're investigating what seems to be a homicide," Tragg said.

"A what?" Mason asked.

"Some fellow out here in Unit 21," Tragg said. "Evidently somebody fed him some Chinese food that was drugged with a barbiturate; and then, when he went to sleep, turned the gas stove on and didn't light it. Occupants of an adjoining unit smelled the gas, called the proprietor, the proprietor got in the door, opened the windows, shut the gas off. It was too late."

"Dead?" Mason asked.

"As a mackerel!" Lieutenant Tragg said. "You wouldn't know anything about it, would you?"

"About the man's death?" Mason asked. "Heavens, no! I had no idea there had been a death until you told me just now."

"Well, I was just checking—that's all," Tragg said. "Sort of a co-incidence, you being here."

He nodded to the driver of the car. "Let's go," he said.

When the police car pulled away, Mason turned back to look at Daphne Shelby.

She was sitting white-faced and frozen, her eyes wide with terror.

"Well?" Mason asked.

She looked at him, tried to say something, then collapsed to the floor of the car.

Mason said, "Inskip will be trailing us because we have Daphne in the car with us. Let's see if we can spot him."

The lawyer made a U-turn, circled back to the corner, suddenly spotted a car parked at the curb, braked his own car to a stop and motioned.

Inskip started the agency car he was driving and pulled alongside.

"Tell Paul we're going back to the Serene Slumber Motel," Mason said. "Tell him to come back there as soon as he finds out what's cooking."

The lawyer drove back to the motel where Daphne had her room. He and Della Street helped Daphne from the car. Daphne handed him the key with cold numb fingers. The lawyer opened the door, escorted Daphne inside.

"All right," Mason said. "Pull yourself together, Daphne. Let's have it straight from the shoulder. Did you have anything to do with your uncle's death?"

She shook her head. Her lips quivered. "I loved him," she said. "He was a father to me. I've sacrificed most of my life trying to make him comfortable."

"That's right," Mason said. "But that's not the way the evidence is going to point."

"What evidence?"

"Let's look at the evidence," Mason said. "You aren't related by blood to Horace Shelby. You can't inherit without a will.

"Shelby's half brother has filed affidavits stating that you are a shrewd and designing person; that you have planned to ingratiate yourself with Horace Shelby and get him to turn his wealth over to you. The records show that Shelby gave you a check for a hundred and twenty-five thousand dollars.

"The Court ordered Shelby to have a conservator for his estate. You smuggled Shelby out of the rest home where he was placed on the orders of a physician, took him to the Northern Lights Motel. You got him to make a will leaving everything to you. And, within hours after he made that will, the man was dead."

"I suppose," she said, "he was so despondent that he *could* have committed suicide, although I would never have thought of it."

"We'll wait until Paul Drake comes," Mason said. "Evidently, the police have reason to believe that barbiturates entered into it. You bought him a Chinese dinner tonight?"

"Yes."

"Brought it in in cardboard containers?"

"Yes."

"And had spoons and ate it from the containers?"

"He liked to use chopsticks," she said. "I bought two pair of chopsticks. We ate it with chopsticks."

"And what did you do with the empty containers?"

"They weren't quite empty," she said. "I had to leave, but Uncle Horace promised he'd flush what was left of the food down the toilet, wash the containers out so they wouldn't smell, and put them in the wastebasket. After all, it isn't a housekeeping unit—just a bedroom—and I thought they might make trouble if he used the wastebasket as a garbage pail."

"There was food left and he promised to flush it down the toilet?"

"Yes."

"Looking at it from the standpoint of the police," Mason said, "they'll claim you did the flushing and it will be considered an attempt to conceal the evidence. Then you weren't content with that, they'll say you washed the cardboard containers out with hot water. You told your uncle to do that?"

"Yes."

"That and the will you let him make out in your favor can send you to the penitentiary for life," the lawyer said.

Drake's code knock sounded on the door.

Della Street let him in.

Drake looked serious.

"How bad is it, Paul?" Mason asked.

"Bad," Drake said.

"Give us the lowdown."

"Someone in Unit 22 had been out to dinner, came home and smelled gas coming from Unit 21. They notified the manager of the motel. He got a passkey and opened the door. The gas just about knocked him down. He opened the door, ran to the windows, opened them, and dragged the man's body out into the open. He notified the police. Police arrived and tried resuscitation. It didn't work."

"Why did they figure homicide instead of suicide?" Mason asked.

"The gas stove is vented," Drake said. "Someone had unscrewed the feed pipe so the gas could escape directly into the room. The guy had been eating Chinese food. The doctor who is riding with the deputy coroner suspected barbiturates. He made a quick test. Apparently, the food was loaded. I think they also found evidence of drugs in the bathroom."

Mason looked at Daphne Shelby.

Her eyes refused to meet his.

"You stayed with your uncle while you both ate Chinese food?" he asked.

"I left before he was finished."

"Did you," he asked, "give him any barbiturates?"

"I—I don't know."

"What do you mean, you don't know?"

"I told you he couldn't sleep without these sleeping pills. He has developed such a need for them that he had to have them. I knew that, so when I left him I gave him the sleeping pills that I had."

"Where did *you* get them?"

"They were given me by a doctor—the same doctor who treats Uncle Horace. You remember when I went away, I was all rundown and nervous. The doctor gave me some sleeping medicine in case I had any trouble sleeping.

"I never needed to use it. From the time I got on that boat, I slept like a log. I felt that Uncle Horace might need those pills, so I gave them to him to use if he needed them."

Mason said, "You have put yourself in a beautiful spot for a first-degree murder rap."

Drake said, "The proprietress of the motel got a little suspicious that everything wasn't quite on the up-and-up. The young woman rented Unit 21 and said her uncle was going to occupy it; that she would bring him in later. She got the license number of her automobile—it was a new Ford."

Mason turned to Daphne and said, "And there you are, Daphne!"

Paul Drake caught Mason's eye; jerked his head, indicating he wanted a private conference.

"Excuse us a moment," Mason said, and walked over to the far corner of the room with the detective.

Drake lowered his voice to a half-whisper. "Look, Perry," he said, "you're in a spot. Your client is in a spot. The minute she produces that will, she's convicted herself of murder.

"That girl isn't any sweet, innocent, naïve rosebud. She's shrewd, scheming and clever.

"She located her uncle. She spirited him out of the institution. She was too smart to put him in the motel where she was staying, but she took him to another motel.

"Everything that she's done indicates that she's quick-thinking and ingenious.

"Now then, she found out that she wasn't actually related to Horace Shelby. She can't get any of his money unless she has a will.

"So she spirits him out from under the hand of the authorities and the guardianship of the Court, gets him to make a will, and then the guy promptly dies.

"Now then, if *you* want to forget about that will, *I'll* forget about it."

"What do you mean?" Mason asked

"It's the strongest single fact against her," Drake said. "Just take that will and burn it up. Have her refrain from mentioning it to anyone, and we can refrain from mentioning it. In that way, we can dispose of some of the worst evidence against her."

Mason shook his head.

"Why not?" Drake asked. "I'll stick my neck out. I'll put my license on the line to give your client a break."

"It isn't that," Mason said. "In the first place, as an officer of the court, I can't tamper with evidence. As a licensed detective, you can't. In the second place, I've always found that truth is the strongest weapon in the arsenal of any attorney. The trouble is lawyers quite frequently don't know what the truth is. They get half-truths from the evidence or from their clients and try to get by on those half-truths.

"As far as we are concerned, we are—"

Mason stopped talking abruptly as heavy steps sounded on the wooden porch of the motel, then knuckles pounded on the door.

Mason said, "Permit me, Daphne." He walked across the room and opened the door.

Lieutenant Tragg, accompanied by a uniformed officer standing on the threshold, had a hard time hiding his surprise.

"What the devil are *you* doing *here?*" Tragg asked.

"Talking with my client," Mason said.

"Well, if your client is the owner of the new Ford automobile out in front, she's going to need an attorney in the worst way," Lieutenant Tragg said.

"Come in," Mason invited. "Daphne, this is Lieutenant Tragg of the Homicide Department. Lieutenant Tragg, Daphne Shelby."

"Oh, ho," Tragg said, "I'm beginning to see a great light. Headquarters tell me they've been looking for Horace Shelby, who was spirited out of the Goodwill Sanitarium despite an order of Court."

Tragg turned to the uniformed officer and said, "Bring in the woman. Let's see if we make an identification."

"Let me point out that that's hardly the best way to make an identification," Mason said.

"Well, it is in this case," Tragg said. "We're working against time."

The officer left the porch, a car door slammed, then there were steps on the porch, and the officer escorted a woman into the motel unit.

"Look around," Tragg invited, "and see if there's anyone here you know."

The woman instantly pointed to Daphne Shelby.

"Why, that's the woman who rented Unit 21," she said. "She told me that her uncle was going to be occupying it."

Tragg turned to Mason with a grin. "This," he said, "is your exit line, Counselor. We can get along without you from here on."

Mason smiled. "I think you're forgetting about the recent Supreme Court decisions, Lieutenant," he said. "Miss Shelby is entitled to have an attorney representing her at *all stages* of the investigation."

Mason turned to Daphne and said, "Before you answer any questions, Daphne, look at me. If I shake my head, don't answer; if I nod my head, answer it and *tell the truth*."

"That's going to be one hell of a way to interrogate a witness," Lieutenant Tragg said.

"It may be a poor way to interrogate a *witness*, but it's the only way you can interrogate a prospective defendant," Mason said. "Perhaps I can make some stipulations which will make things easier for you, Lieutenant."

"Such as what?" Tragg asked.

"This is Daphne Shelby," Mason said. "Until a short time ago, she believed in good faith that she was the niece of Horace Shelby.

"However, whether there is any blood relationship or not, Daphne is very fond of the man she has always regarded as her uncle. She lived in the house and took charge of his rather restricted diet. She was on the verge of a nervous breakdown from trying to nurse him, do the cooking, and supervise the housekeeping problems.

"When Horace Shelby was sent to the Goodwill Sanitarium by a conservator and a doctor who was employed by the other relatives, Daphne obtained employment at the sanitarium. She found Horace Shelby strapped to a bed, she took a knife, cut the straps, took Horace Shelby to the Northern Lights Motel and established him in Unit 21.

"Now then, Lieutenant, that's as far as we are going to go at the present time."

Tragg whirled to Daphne. "Did you bring him some food tonight?"

Mason shook his head.

Daphne remained quiet.

"Chinese food in particular," Lieutenant Tragg said. "We know you did so you might just as well make it easy on yourself. After all,

Miss Shelby, we're trying to get at the truth in the case; and, if you're innocent, you have nothing to fear from the truth."

Again Mason shook his head.

"Shucks," Tragg muttered, then turned to Mason. "Any objection to letting her identify the body?"

"None whatever," Mason said.

Tragg turned to Daphne Shelby and held out his hand. "Would you mind giving me those sleeping pills you have, Miss Shelby?" he asked. "The ones you've got left."

She started to reach for her purse, then caught Mason's eye.

"No dice, Lieutenant," Mason said. "We don't want to have you resort to subterfuge because, under those circumstances, we might quit co-operating."

Lieutenant Tragg said bitterly, "It's one hell of a note when the Court takes the handcuffs off the defendant and puts them on the wrists of honest officers who are trying to enforce the law."

"I don't see any handcuffs," Mason said.

"Well, I can *feel* them," Tragg snapped.

"We were going to identify a body," Mason reminded him.

"All right, come on," Tragg said; and then added, "We're going to have to deprive you of that Ford automobile for a while, Miss Shelby. It's evidence, and we've got to have it identified."

"That's all right," Mason said. "We're co-operating in every way we can in the investigation."

"Yes," Tragg said, drawing his extended forefinger across his throat. "I can feel the cordiality of your co-operation."

Tragg turned to the officer, said, "Call in on the radio. Have a fingerprint expert come out and check that Ford car for fingerprints."

He turned to Daphne and said, "You come with me."

"I'll ride in the car with you," Mason said.

Tragg shook his head.

"Then Daphne rides with me," Mason announced.

Tragg thought things over, then said, "All right, Daphne rides with you. You follow me."

"I'll tag along behind to make the procession complete," Drake added.

"Come on, Della, you and Daphne sit in the back seat of my car," Mason instructed.

"Daphne, you're not to answer any questions by anyone unless I am present and advise you to answer. Do you understand?"

She nodded.

"Now, you're in for a shock," Mason said in a low voice. "They're going to take you to identify your uncle's body. You can make the identification, that's all. I don't want you to volunteer any information or answer any questions, do you understand?"

She nodded in a tight-lipped silence.

"This is going to be a very harrowing experience," Mason said, "and you've had plenty of them within the last twenty-four hours. But you're going to have to brace yourself and bear up.

"All right, Lieutenant, let's go."

The cars made a procession down the road until they came to the Northern Lights Motel.

A stretcher wagon was waiting to take the remains to the morgue for autopsy.

Lieutenant Tragg walked over to the stretcher, took hold of a corner of the blanket and said, "This way, please, Miss Shelby."

She came to stand by the officer. Mason stood at her side, holding her arm.

Tragg jerked back the blanket.

Suddenly, Mason felt Daphne stiffen. She clutched at the lawyer, then gave a half scream.

Mason patted her shoulder.

"That isn't Uncle Horace," she said. "That's Ralph Exeter!"

Lieutenant Tragg was puzzled. "Who's Ralph Exeter?" he asked.

Daphne's numb lips made two futile attempts before words came. "A friend of Uncle Borden."

"And who's Uncle Borden?"

"A half brother of Horace Shelby."

"Then how did Exeter get in this unit of the motel and where is Horace Shelby now?"

Mason said, "Those are two questions, Lieutenant, which you are going to have to answer all by yourself."

The woman who had identified Daphne Shelby came over to the officers. "Want to take a look?" Lieutenant Tragg asked her.

She nodded.

Tragg drew back the blanket.

"I don't think that's the man who's supposed to be in Unit 21!"

she said. "It look like the man who rented Unit 20 about three hours ago."

"How did he come here?" Tragg asked.

"He had his own car. It had a Massachusetts license. There may have been someone with him—a woman. I can get the registration card."

"*We'll* get it," Tragg said.

He accompanied her to the office, came back holding the registration card.

"That's right," he said. "He registered under his own name. He gave the license number of his car—a Massachsetts license number.

"Now then, where's his car? What became of it? It isn't here."

There was an interval of silence, then Tragg said, "Let's take a look in Unit 20 and see what we find in there."

He turned to Mason. "Since you aren't of any help in this phase of the investigation, you and your client can go, but I want both of you to be available where I can reach you on short notice."

Mason said, "Excuse me a minute, Daphne. It will only take a moment."

The lawyer moved over to Paul Drake, lowered his voice, said, "Paul, Horace Shelby was in that cabin. He isn't there now. He left under his own power or he was taken away.

"If he was taken away, we're in trouble. If he left under his own power, I'd like to make sure that he's on his own and see if we take steps to keep him on his own."

Drake nodded.

"Start your men covering the taxicab companies right away," Mason said.

Again Drake nodded.

"Now then," Mason went on, "it would be fatal if the police managed to implant in the proprietress' mind the idea that Ralph Exeter was the man Daphne brought to the motel.

"She's seen Daphne. She identified the license number of the car Daphne was driving, and she's identified Daphne.

"Get to work on her in advance of the police. Get her to state that she can't identify the woman who was with Exeter in the car in which Exeter arrived at the motel. And be darned sure to tie her up so that she can't testify later on that the more she thinks of it, the more she believes Daphne was the one who was in Exeter's car.

"You know and I know that personal identification evidence is just about the worst, the most unreliable type of evidence we have—not when a person identifies someone he knows but when he gets a glimpse of an individual and then later on makes an identification—either from a photograph or from personal contact."

"Sure, we all know that," Drake said. "I'll do what I can. Anything else?"

"That's all," Mason said. "Get your men working. Use that telephone in your car. Put your men out and get busy on that woman while Lieutenant Tragg is searching Unit 20 for clues."

"On my way," Drake said. "Which comes first?"

"The talk with the proprietress of the motel," Mason told him. "We don't know how long Lieutenant Tragg is going to be in Unit 20. You can telephone the taxicab companies shortly after that."

Chapter TWELVE

Mason put an arm around Daphne Shelby, drew her over to his car, felt her trembling like a leaf beneath her coat.

"Take it easy, Daphne! Take it easy!" the lawyer warned. "We're running up against something that may be pretty complicated. This man was found in Unit 21. Now, that's the unit you rented for your uncle?"

She nodded.

The lawyer escorted her into the back seat of his car, had Della Street move in on the other side, said to Daphne, "You went to the Chinese restaurant and got Chinese food to take out?"

"Yes."

"Who waited on you?"

"Heavens, I don't know. It was some girl."

"Not Chinese?"

"No. The cook was Chinese."

"How did you happen to go to that restaurant?"

She pointed and said, "You can see the sign there—right over there."

Mason followed the direction of her finger and saw the big illuminated sign in green letters reading CHINESE COOKING.

Mason said, "When Lieutenant Tragg asked you for the sleeping pills you had, you started to open your purse."

She nodded.

"You have sleeping pills in there?"

"No, it was because he extended his hand and acted the way he did. I forgot for the moment that I had given the sleeping pills to Uncle Horace."

"Keep on forgetting it for the time being," Mason said. "Don't answer any questions about the sleeping pills.

"Now then, Exeter checked into this motel sometime this evening. That means that they knew where you had placed Uncle Horace and were just biding their time."

"Then why didn't they get officers and take him back to the sanitarium?" she asked. "That's what both Uncle Horace and I were afraid of."

"Probably because they were afraid that the Court-appointed doctor would then examine him, and they wanted to work him over a little bit before they let Dr. Alma get in touch with him."

"Then you think they have Uncle Horace with them?"

"It's a very distinct possibility," Mason said.

"What will happen now?" she asked.

Mason said, "They'll get him all doped up. They'll terrify him. They will then return him to the sanitarium and notify Dr. Alma."

"Is there any way of counteracting that?" she asked. "Is there anything we can do? Any way we can find Uncle Horace?"

"I really don't know," Mason said, "but we have two alternatives to consider."

"What are those?"

"One," Mason said, is that your Uncle Horace left here with Borden Finchley. But somehow I don't subscribe to that theory."

"What's the other alternative?"

"That he left here under his own power and of his own volition."

"But why would he leave here?" she asked.

Mason looked her straight in the eyes. "Because he had killed Ralph Exeter."

"Why, Uncle Horace wouldn't . . ." Her voice trailed off into silence.

"Exactly," Mason said. "You don't know *all* the details about how your Uncle Horace has been treated. You don't know his mental

condition. You gave him sleeping pills. Suppose Exeter had the adjoining room; then, after you had left the motel, Exeter walked into
Horace Shelby's room and started making demands on him.

"Remember that Exeter wasn't really Bordon Finchley's friend.
He was only interested in getting money, and the money had to
come from Horace Shelby.

"So suppose Exeter demanded a hundred and twenty-five thousand dollars from Horace Shelby as the price of his co-operation.
Suppose Exeter said he hadn't had anything to eat and started to help
himself to the rest of the food in the containers.

"Horace wanted to get rid of the man. He simply dumped the
sleeping medicine into the Chinese food. He could have mashed the
pills up into a powder while Exeter was talking.

"Perhaps his original intention was to drug Exeter into insensibil-
ity and then escape. But after he saw Exeter lying there helpless, he
may have decided to make a permanent job of it."

She shook her head. "Not Uncle Horace. He wouldn't do anything like that. He wouldn't kill a fly."

"Then," Mason said, "unless we can involve Borden Finchley,
there's only one other suspect."

"Who?"

"You," Mason said.

"Me?"

Mason nodded.

She shook her head and said, "This is what Uncle Borden would
have done, but not what I would have done and not what Uncle
Horace would have done."

"We'll also investigate your Uncle Borden," Mason said.

"When?" she asked.

"Now," Mason said and, putting his car into gear, drove out of the
motel parking lot.

"What am I to do?" Daphne asked.

"You," Mason said, "are going to go back to your hotel and stay
there. If you cut any more capers or have any more unauthorized
absences, you're going to find yourself charged with murder."

"Ralph Exeter?"

"Yes."

"But why in the world should I have murdered him?"

"I can think of half a dozen reasons," Mason said. "One of them is that he is the moving force against your Uncle Horace. He was the one who was putting on the pressure. And if I can think of one good motive, the police can think of a dozen.

"You aren't out of the woods yet, young lady. You're suspect right now. There *are* those who think that underneath that shell of cherubic innocence you're a shrewd, scheming individual trying to look out for your own future at all costs."

She said, "I've been perfectly frank with you, Mr. Mason."

"Yes, I know," the lawyer said. "You've told me all the things you wanted me to know. You've put all the cards on the table that you wanted me to see. But I'd feel a lot better about you, Daphne, if you hadn't sneaked out of that hotel, shown such ingenuity in going to that sanitarium and getting a job, then spiriting your uncle out of there.

"I don't know whether you're doing it for you or doing it for him, but you certainly aren't being very considerate of me.

"I stuck my neck out getting some money for you, and I'm entitled to your co-operation."

"I know," she said quietly. "And don't think I don't appreciate all you've done."

"If you gave that money back to your uncle," Mason said, "it's one of the good things to be put on the credit side of the ledger as far as you're concerned. But don't kid yourself, before the night is over the police are going to be hot on your trail.

"If they call on you, I want you to insist that you telephone me. I'll give you a night number where I can be reached. Don't answer any questions, under any circumstances, until I get there.

"And, in the meantime, don't question anything that I do."

"Why should I question anything that you do?" she asked.

"Because," Mason told her, "if I have the chance, I'm going to use your Uncle Horace as a red herring."

"What do you mean 'a red herring'?"

Mason said, "I'm going to let the police get the idea that your Uncle Horace murdered Ralph Exeter, and that he was medically if not legally insane at the time he did it."

Chapter THIRTEEN

It was well after ten o'clock that evening when Paul Drake's code knock sounded on the door of Mason's office.

Della Street opened the door.

A bedraggled Paul Drake, his face oily with weariness, came in, slumped into a chair, said, "I tried to make it sooner. I knew you people wanted to go home, but it's been one hell of a job."

"What did you find out?" Mason asked.

"Something that the police have been suppressing," Drake said. "I found out how they really knew about the barbiturates."

"How come?"

Drake said, "In the bathroom in the apartment where they found the man lying dead—Unit 21 of the motel—they found a tumbler, one of those heavy glass tumblers that go with motel rooms, you know the kind they wrap in a wax paper package with an antiseptic label."

Mason nodded.

"Inside the tumbler was the glass tube of a toothbrush case and a little white powder," Drake said. "Lieutenant Tragg treated the glass for fingerprints."

"Did he get any?"

"He got some prints. Probably those of Horace Shelby, but they don't know for sure."

"Go ahead," Mason said.

"Someone had used the glass tube of the toothbrush case to grind up some sleeping pills, using the tumbler as an impromptu mortar, and the toothbrush case as an improvised pestle."

"How do they know about the toothbrush case having been used as a pestle?"

"Some of the powder had been ground into the rounded end of the glass case hard enough so it stuck there."

"Tragg's a thorough cuss," Mason said.

Drake nodded.

"What was the powder?" Mason asked.

"It's a barbiturate preparation called Somniferone. It's a combination preparation that is very quick in its action and is combined with another barbiturate derivative which is more lasting. The result is a combination which takes effect quickly and lasts a long time."

"How'd they get it identified?" Mason asked.

"One of these X-ray analytical machines. Tragg got fingerprints from the glass and then rushed the whole thing up to the police laboratory."

"All right," Mason said, "I can see you're leading up to something. Hand it to me."

"Somniferone," Drake said, "is the barbiturate that was prescribed for Horace Shelby by the doctor who was called in by Borden Finchley after they moved in. He is the same doctor who prescribed the sedative for Daphne to take with her on her long ocean voyage—and just before she left they filled the prescription for her. She had a whole three months' supply of Somniferone."

"Go on," Mason said.

"The police don't know it yet, but they're investigating," Drake said. "They're getting on the right track."

"What's the right track?"

"Your client," Drake said. "That girl certainly can put on an act. She poses as little Miss Sweetness, little Miss Innocence, but she's a deep one."

"What did she do?" Mason asked.

"She went to a Chinese restaurant. She got some Chinese food. She went to Unit 21. She took her sleeping pills and ground them up in the glass tumbler with the toothbrush case. She invited Ralph Exeter in for a conference. She drugged his food, dumped all the food that was uneaten down the toilet and washed out the pasteboard containers. After he slipped into a drugged sleep, she disconnected the gas pipe so the gas was on, and left. She knew that, one way or another, she wasn't going to be bothered any more with Ralph Exeter."

Mason shook his head. "I won't buy it, Paul."

"You don't have to buy it," Drake said. "The police are going to buy it."

"She bought the Chinese food for Horace Shelby," Mason said.

"No she didn't," Drake said. "Shelby was long gone."

"What do you mean?"

"We've found a cabdriver who received a call to pick up a passenger at the street corner where the Northern Lights Motel is located.

"He went there. An elderly man, who seemed somewhat confused, was waiting. He got in the cab and seemed a little uncertain about where he wanted to go. He started for the Union Station; then changed his mind and said he'd go to the airport. The cab took him to the airport. The man seemed to be loaded with cash. He took a roll of bills from his pocket. A hundred-dollar bill was the smallest he had. The cabdriver had to go with him into the airport to get the bill changed.

"That man was Horace Shelby. The description fits."

"The time element?" Mason asked.

"The time element was a good hour before Daphne went to the Chinese restaurant, got the food in pasteboard containers; then went to the Northern Lights Motel."

"All right," Mason said, "that's circumstantial evidence, but we haven't got all the evidence yet, Paul. Daphne didn't have any motive for killing Ralph Exeter."

"Don't kid yourself," Drake said. "She was more resentful of Ralph than of anyone in the crowd. She regarded Borden Finchley as her uncle and Borden's wife was her aunt. Exeter was the one who was making the trouble, putting on all the pressure, and she knew it."

"What about Borden Finchley?" Mason asked. "Where was he while all this was going on?"

"Borden Finchley has an alibi. So does his wife, Elinor."

"You've checked?"

"I've checked. Of course, it's a husband-and-wife affair in part, but there's some independent corroboration. The Finchleys were moving all of Daphne's things out of her room, taking an inventory of every garment, every jar of toilet preparations, every paper. They were at it for three hours.

"The housekeeper was downstairs most of the time, crying over what was happening. Mrs. Finchley came downstairs for something and gave the housekeeper a tongue-lashing and sent her home."

Mason said, "There were men from Las Vegas who were interested, Paul. When I made my first visit to the Goodwill Sanitarium, a man came up to the car and asked me if I was the doctor the Court had appointed to examine Horace Shelby. I told him I wasn't. The man hurriedly walked away, got into a car which was parked some distance ahead and drove off.

"I couldn't make out the license number but I could see it was a Nevada license plate. I could tell by the colors. I didn't want to be too obvious about trying to follow him, because I felt they might be watching in the rearview mirror, so I made a play of starting to go to the sanitarium; then changing my mind. I took out after them to try and get the license number. I never did find them. I must have lost them at an intersection."

"Could be, all right," Drake said, "but at the time your client was in Unit 21 at the Northern Lights Motel apparently taking food to Horace Shelby, Horace Shelby had been long gone."

"No question about the time element?"

Drake shook his head, "No question."

Mason said, "All right, Paul, we're going to have a showdown with Daphne. She's held out on me too often and too much."

Mason nodded to Della Street. "Get her on the phone," he said.

Della Street checked the number on the card she had, sent her fingers spinning over the dial, gave the number of Daphne's room and said, "I'd like to speak with Miss Shelby, please."

She waited a moment, then said, "The poor kid's probably asleep. She's certainly had a day."

"Poor kid, my eye," Drake said. "That girl is probably up to some skulduggery right now."

The three of them sat waiting in tense expectancy.

After a while, Della Street said, "Are you certain you're ringing the right room, Operator? Would you mind trying it again just to make sure?"

Again there was a period of silence and Della Street said, "Thank you, we'll call later. No message."

She hung up the telephone and said, "No answer. She's either not in her room or . . ."

Her voice trailed away into silence.

Perry Mason got up from his chair, nodded to Drake. "Okay, folks," he said, "let's go."

"One car?" Drake asked, as they descended in the elevator.

"Taxicab," Mason said tersely. "I don't want a parking problem when we get there, and we can get plenty of cabs in front of the hotel when we want to come back."

They emerged from Mason's office building, found a cab parked at the cabstand a few steps from the entrance and the three of them piled in.

Mason gave the driver the name of Daphne's hotel, and the driver made a quick run, getting there within a matter of seven or eight minutes.

The lawyer gave him a liberal tip, entered the hotel and with complete assurance walked to the elevator, said, "Seventh floor," to the elevator operator, and when they left the elevator the lawyer turned to the left, strode down the corridor.

The elevator doors closed.

Mason waited until the operator had moved the cage from the seventh floor before looking at the numbers on the rooms, then turned abruptly. "Wrong direction," he said. "I didn't want the elevator boy to know we weren't oriented."

"What's the number?" Drake asked.

"Seven eighteen," Mason said.

They retraced their steps, found 718.

There was a sign on the door, DO NOT DISTURB.

Della Street said, "Let's take one thing into consideration. The poor kid was up all last night, working in that sanitarium. She's gone for thirty-six hours without sleep. It's only natural she should put a *Do Not Disturb* sign on the door and go to bed."

"Also it's only natural that she should wake up to answer the telephone," Mason said.

"Perhaps not if she's sleeping the sleep of exhaustion," Della Street said.

Mason's knuckles banged on the door.

The lawyer waited for a moment; then knocked loudly for a second time. There was no answer.

Mason said, "Della, I hate to ask you to do this, but I want to see the inside of that room.

"Go down on the elevator, leave the hotel; then reenter, walk boldly up to the clerk's desk and ask him for the key to 718.

"If you have just the right amount of assurance, just the right poise, he'll hand the key to you. If he asks you your name, tell him Daphne Shelby. If he goes any further and asks for identification, tell him who you are, tell him I'm waiting up here; that Daphne is my client; that I'm afraid she's been drugged or perhaps murdered and is not answering the door because she can't answer the door.

"If it comes to that, ask the house detective to accompany you up here."

"Chief, do you really think she's—"

"How do I know?" Mason said. "We've had one murder. We could have two. What I'm telling you now is the attitude you're to adopt with the house detective if necessary. Tell him I'm waiting up here with a private detective. That will take you off the spot for trying to get the key to another person's room."

Della Street nodded.

"Think you can do it?" Mason asked.

"I can make one of the best attempts that you ever saw," she said, smiling.

"Try to leave the lobby unostentatiously so the clerk won't notice you going out. When you come in, just ask for the key."

"But suppose Daphne has the key with her?"

"These hotels nearly always have two keys to a room in the pigeonhole, and a third key in a drawer that they can open in case the other keys are lost."

Della Street said, "You'll be here?"

"We'll be here," Mason said.

Della Street walked to the elevator, rang the button, and a moment later was taken down.

Mason, simply as a matter of precaution, tapped on the door again.

When he had no answer, he turned, leaned against the wall with his shoulders and hips, elevated his right foot so that it was flat against the wall and said to the detective, "We have more damned complications."

"Depending, of course, on what has happened," Drake said.

"No matter what's happened," Mason said, "we've got complications. If she's in and doesn't answer the door or the telephone, we've probably got a corpse—or perhaps someone who has been drugged with a barbiturate. In that case our only hope is that we can rush her to the hospital and save her life.

"If she *isn't* in her room, we've got real problems."

"Such as what?"

"Suppose Lieutenant Tragg wants to question her. He told her not to leave town, to keep herself available for questions. If she's not in her room, Tragg will regard that as flight, and in this state, flight is evidence of guilt."

"Oh, oh!" Drake said.

They waited for some four or five minutes, and then the elevator stopped again at the seventh floor. The doors slid back, and Della Street nodded her thanks to the operator and started walking rapidly toward them.

"Do any good?" Mason asked.

By way of answer, Della Street exhibited the key with the metallic oval tag fastened to it by a ring.

She fitted the key in the door.

"Better let me do this," Mason said, stepping forward. "If the door is bolted from the inside, it means we've got a major problem. If it isn't bolted, I'm her attorney and I'd better be the one that opens the door."

The key clicked back the latch. Mason tentatively tried the door, turned the knob, pushed against the door, then put his shoulder against it.

Mason turned to the others.

"That does it," he said. "It's bolted from the inside."

"That means she's in there?"

The lawyer nodded.

Drake said, "Let's get the house detective."

"We'll try one more time," Mason said.

This time his knuckles pounded a double tattoo on the panels of the door.

"All right," Mason said, "we've got to get the detective and force the door. We . . ."

The lawyer broke off as there was the sound of a bolt being moved on the inside of the door.

The bolt on the inside of the door slid all the way back, and the door opened.

Daphne Shelby in a sheer nightgown stood sleepily regarding them.

"What . . . I'm dizzy . . . Help . . ." She collapsed to the floor.

Della Street ran to her side.

Mason said, "There's a house physician here. Let's get him. But first, keep her from going to sleep. Paul, get some cold compresses. Put them on her head and neck."

Drake said, "Okay, let's lift her back into bed and—"

"Not bed," Mason said. "That's the worst place for her if she's been drugged. Keep her walking. I'll take one side, Della can take the other. Keep her moving. Get some cold towels."

"I'll get a wrap of some sort," Della said.

She hurried to the closet, came out with a wrap, and the three of them managed to get the garment around the girl. Then Mason and Della started her walking. Drake hurried into the bathroom.

Daphne took one or two steps, then suddenly slumped, moaned and said, "Oh, I'm so sleepy . . . so, so . . . so sleepy."

Drake came hurrying out of the bathroom with a cold towel. He put it on Daphne's neck; then on her head. "Come on, Daphne," he said, "keep walking."

Mason said, "What happened, Daphne?"

"I think I'm poisoned," she said sleepily.

"I know. What makes you think you're poisoned?"

"I stopped at the lunch counter. I had some chocolate. That was all I wanted, just a big pot of hot chocolate and some toast. I was so tired. I'd been up all night."

"I know," Mason said, "go on."

"The chocolate tasted funny," she said, and then added, "I had gone to the telephone and left it there for a minute. I asked the waitress not to take it away. There was a funny-looking woman sitting next to the end . . ." Abruptly Daphne ceased talking and became a dead weight.

Mason and Della Street got her to her feet. Drake appeared with another cold towel. Mason said, "Get on the phone, Paul. Get the house doctor up here on the double. Tell him we have a sleeping pill case."

Mason pulled back the robe, shoved the cold towel down Daphne's spine.

"Ooooh," she exclaimed, giving a little jump. "That's cold."

"It'll do you good," Mason said, "Keep walking."

"I . . . can't . . . walk . . . I want to lie down and go . . . sleep

"Keep walking," Mason said. "Keep walking."

Drake turned from the telephone. "A doctor will be on his way up here inside of a few seconds."

Mason nodded to Della Street. "Get Room Service, Della, tell them to send up two pots of strong black coffee."

"Please let me . . . go . . . ," Daphne said.

"Keep the towels coming, Paul," Mason ordered.

"No, no," she protested listlessly, "I'm sopping wet!"

Mason said, "You'll *be* wet when *we* get done here. . . . Paul, fill the bathtub full of water that's just a little bit warmer than lukewarm. Della Street can see that she gets a tepid bath—just enough to give her a little stimulation and keep her from getting chilled. We want it just a few degrees warmer than body temperature."

Drake handed Mason two more cold towels, said, "I wish I had four hands."

Mason kept Daphne walking. Della Street ordered black coffee. From the bathroom was the sound of running water.

Daphne sighed. Her head fell over on Mason's shoulder and again she slumped.

The lawyer elevated her to her feet.

"Walk," Mason said, "walk, Daphne. You've *got* to help. You've got to walk. I can't just carry you by your arms. Walk!"

"I can't feel the floor," she said. "My feet aren't touching anything."

"Do you think the woman sitting next to you put something in your chocolate?"

"It tasted funny, sort of bitter, but I put more sugar in it."

"Can you describe her? Do you know what she looked like?" Mason asked.

"No . . . I can't concentrate . . . I'm sorry to let you down like this, Mr. Mason."

Again her legs seemed to buckle.

Mason and Della lifted the dead weight.

Mason pulled back his left hand, and with the palm gave Daphne's rump a sharp slap.

Her back arched as she jerked her hips out of the way.

"Don't you ever do that again!" she blazed, and then suddenly moaned and again collapsed.

This time neither the lawyer nor Della Street could get her to make any effort to stand on her feet. She simply remained a dead weight.

Mason stood looking down at her with thought-slitted eyes, then said to Della Street, "Let's put her over on the bed."

"But she'll just go into unconsciousness," Della Street said. "You told us that yourself, Perry."

"I know," Mason said. "Get her over on the bed."

There was a knock at the door.

Drake opened it.

A professional-appearing man with a black medical bag said, "I'm Dr. Selkirk."

Mason said, "This young woman seems to have been given an overdose of barbiturates."

"All right," Dr. Selkirk said, "we'll pump her stomach out."

"And let's save what we get," Mason said, "I'm interested."

"Any container around here?" Dr. Selkirk asked.

Mason said, "There's a water pitcher."

"Well, that'll do if we have to use it."

Dr. Selkirk said, "We need some coffee."

"It's been ordered," Mason said.

"And we'll cover her up and keep her warm."

The physician pumped out the contents of the stomach; then listened with a stethoscope at the girl's chest. He frowned, took her pulse, then went over the pitcher containing the contents of the stomach.

Mason stepped into the bathroom, said to Paul Drake, "Get that water just as ice cold as you can get it, Paul."

"What?" Drake asked, incredulously.

"Just as cold as you can get it."

Dr. Selkirk motioned to Perry Mason. "May I see you a minute?" he asked.

Mason moved over to him. Dr. Selkirk lowered his voice, glanced apprehensively over his shoulder to where Della Street was smoothing Daphne's wet hair back from her forehead.

"There's something funny about this," Dr. Selkirk said. "Her pulse is strong and active, her respiration is normal and regular, but there are remains in the stomach contents that are pills, all right."

"You mean the pills haven't digested? Did she swallow them in the chocolate?" Mason asked.

"She's had chocolate within the last hour or so," Dr. Selkirk said, "but I doubt if the pills were ingested at the same time as the chocolate. I think that they were taken later."

Mason said, "Would it be all right if I tried an experiment, Doctor?"

"What sort of an experiment?"

Mason raised his voice. "I've instructed Mr. Drake here, a private investigator, to fill the bathtub with warm water, I want to . . ."

Dr. Selkirk started shaking his head.

"I want to keep her from getting chilled by putting her in this warm water," Mason said.

Dr. Selkirk started to say something.

Mason raised a finger to catch Dr. Selkirk's attention; then closed his eye in an unmistakable wink.

"Come on, Della," Mason said, "get her in the bathroom. We'll help you if necessary. Let her soak in that water for about ten minutes."

"She'll relax and go right to sleep, probably into a deep stupor," Dr. Selkirk said.

"Let's try it, anyway," Mason said. "We can always pull her out."

"I'm not going to strip the clothes off her," Della said angrily. "You should have a nurse if you want—"

"That's all right," Mason said, "leave her clothes on, that is, *both* the robe and the nightdress, just dunk her in that warm water."

Della said, "You'll have to help me."

"I'll help you," Mason said.

They picked Daphne up, carried her to the door of the bathroom, swung her around over the bath water.

"Are you awake, Daphne?" Mason asked.

The eyelids fluttered, but there was no other motion.

"All right," Mason said, "drop her, Della."

Mason let go of the shoulders, and Della Street let go of the feet. The girl splashed into the bathtub.

There was a shrill scream. Daphne exclaimed, "What the hell do you think you're doing!" and came up out of the bathtub, pushing, clawing, fighting mad. "That water's ice cold!" she screamed. "You son of a—"

"All right, Daphne," Mason interrupted. "It was a good try but it didn't work. Della will stay in here with you and help get you dry and bring you some clothes from the closet; then perhaps you can come out and tell us what this is *really* all about."

Mason stepped out and closed the door.

"I'm freezing," Daphne said as the door closed.

"Get those things off," Della ordered.

"Put some hot water in that tub. Get me a hot shower. I'm frozen to the bone."

Drake said, "How the hell did you know, Perry?"

Mason said, "The first two steps she took when we started walking her were perfectly normal steps; then she suddenly remembered and took all the spring out of her legs. A moment later, she was a dead weight. Then she came to again and tried it some more. She did a pretty fair job, but she didn't know just what she was doing."

"What about these stomach contents?" Dr. Selkirk asked.

"Forget them," Mason said. "Flush them down the toilet and send me your bill, Doctor. I'm Perry Mason, the lawyer. I've found out all I want to know."

"That was pretty strenuous treatment, a girl who expects to be immersed in warm water suddenly finding herself plunged into a bathtub full of ice cold water . . ."

"I felt there'd be a reaction." Mason grinned. "But I didn't think it would be quite as . . ."

He broke off as knuckles sounded on the door.

Dr. Selkirk looked questioningly at Mason.

"This is the girl's room," Mason said hastily. "I don't think we should answer the door."

The knocking became peremptory. Lieutenant Tragg's voice called out, "Open up. This is the law!"

Mason shrugged his shoulders.

Dr. Selkirk said, "I'm house physician here at the hotel. We have to recognize a summons of that sort."

He walked across and opened the door.

Tragg showed surprise. "Is a Miss Daphne Shelby in here?" he asked. And then, suddenly catching sight of Perry Mason, said, "Well, for heaven's sake, what are *you* doing here?"

Mason said, "Miss Shelby is ill. She's been poisoned with barbiturates. Della Street is with her in the bathroom. I want to talk with her when she comes out."

"And I want to talk with her," Lieutenant Tragg said.

He turned to Dr. Selkirk. "Who are you?"

"I'm Dr. Selkirk, the house physician."

"What's the matter with her?"

Mason said, "You have treated her as a professional man, Doctor. You should have the consent of the patient, I believe, before answering that question."

Dr. Selkirk hesitated.

Tragg said, "Don't let that sharp lawyer bamboozle you. Did she call you?"

"Somebody called me from this room," Dr. Selkirk said.

"You're the house physician?"

"Yes."

"You're representing the hotel," Tragg said. "What's the matter with her?"

"I . . . I'm not prepared to state at this moment."

Tragg walked over to the pitcher which was on the floor by the bed.

"What's this?" he asked.

"Contents we pumped out of her stomach."

"What are these pink things?" Tragg asked.

"Pills. Pills which have become partially dissolved."

"Somebody tried to give her a drug?" Tragg asked.

"That was the reason I had the stomach contents pumped out," Dr. Selkirk said, then hesitated.

"Well, I'll be darned," Tragg said.

"However," Dr. Selkirk went on, "I would say that those pills had been ingested within the last fifteen minutes. We've been here almost that long. It is my considered professional opinion that those pills were ingested just before she opened the door to let these gentlemen in."

A triumphant smile spread over Tragg's face.

"Now that," he said, "is exactly the type of evidence I was looking for. I didn't know whether we'd find it so easy, but—"

"Well, *what* do you know!"

Mason said, "Are you absolutely certain of your diagnosis, Doctor?"

Dr. Selkirk grinned. "You seemed to be absolutely certain of yours."

Mason stepped to the door of the bathroom, said, "Lieutenant Tragg is here. He's going to ask some questions, Daphne, and I don't want you to answer a single question, not a word."

"Now, wait a minute," Tragg said, "tactics such as those are going to be responsible for making a lot of trouble for this young lady."

"What sort of trouble?"

"I'll take her up to Headquarters."

"Under arrest?"

"Possibly."

"You won't take her from here unless you do arrest her," Mason said; and then added, "And if you arrest her, your face is going to be awfully red if you have to back up in the light of subsequently discovered evidence."

Tragg thought things over for a moment, then walked over to the most comfortable chair in the room and seated himself.

"Doctor," he said to Dr. Selkirk, "I don't want you to talk with anyone until I've had a chance to ask you some questions about this case. You may as well go now, if you think there's no danger."

"No danger whatever," Dr. Selkirk said. "Her pulse is strong and regular, just a little rapid. Apparently she's under some excitement. Her heartbeat is strong and clear. Her respiration is perfect. The pupils of her eyes react normally. Her stomach has been pumped out, and any barbiturates she may have taken will perhaps help her to get a good night's sleep, but they aren't in the least dangerous."

Tragg went over to the writing desk, folded a piece of stationery so it came to a sharp point and started fishing the pills out of the liquid in the water pitcher.

"Rather a dirty job," he said, "but I think this is going to be evidence, the sort of evidence I've been looking for."

Della Street called out from the bathroom, "Will you hand me in the clothes that are on the chair by the bed?"

Mason crossed over to the chair, picked up the clothes which had been piled helter-skelter on the chair, knocked on the bathroom door.

Della Street opened it a crack, and Mason passed the clothes in.

Tragg said, "Perry, I'm going to take this girl down to Headquarters. If I have to, I'll arrest her on suspicion of murder. I have enough evidence to justify what I'm doing."

"Go right ahead," Mason said, "but I'll instruct her to answer no questions unless I'm present. This girl has been up all night. Why don't you let her have a night's sleep and interrogate her tomorrow?"

"We will," Tragg promised, "but she's going to have that night's sleep where we can be pretty darned sure she doesn't gobble another dose of sleeping pills."

"Have it your own way," Mason said.

Tragg looked at him thoughtfully and said, "There's something going on in that brain of yours, Perry. What is it?"

Mason said, "Simply the feeling that you're making trouble for yourself, taking irrevocable steps before you're sure of what you're doing."

"You worry about your problems and I'll worry about mine," Tragg said.

After a few minutes, Della Street and Daphne emerged from the bathroom.

"I'm sorry, Daphne," Lieutenant Tragg said, "but you're going to have to go up to Headquarters. I'm going to keep you tonight where I can be sure I can put my finger on you in the morning. I've promised Perry Mason that I'm going to let you get a night's sleep and I will, but I'm also going to see to it that you don't take any more sleeping pills.

"Now, how many did you take?"

"Don't answer any questions," Mason said.

Tragg sighed. "All right," he said, "bring your things. I'm not going to try to search your purse here, but I warn you that when we get to the detention ward all of your possessions will be searched. Then you'll be given prison clothes and no sleeping pills."

Daphne, her head erect, her eyes flashing, marched toward the door, turned to Perry Mason and said, "Mr. Smarty Pants! You with your cold water!"

Mason warned, "Be your age, Daphne. I'm trying to help you. Your own efforts are amateurish."

"Well, yours are *thoroughly* professional and disgusting," she snapped.

Lieutenant Tragg listened curiously. "All right, Daphne," he said, at length, "let's go."

They left the room.

Perry Mason said in a low voice, "Keep your key, Della."

They all rode down in the elevator. Tragg hustled Daphne across the lobby and into a police car.

Mason said hurriedly, "Let's go back up to Daphne's room. Hurry!"

"Why?" Drake asked.

"Why do you think Daphne took those sleeping pills?" Mason asked.

"To arouse sympathy; to make it appear someone else was passing out the drugs?"

Mason shook his head. "We trapped her when we knocked on the door. She didn't dare come to the door until she'd jumped out of her clothes into a nightie, gulped down some sleeping pills and decided to put on the act."

"Why?" Della Street asked.

"To keep us from speculating on what she'd been doing while we were knocking on the door and waiting."

"What had she been doing?"

"Unless I miss my guess very much indeed," Mason said, "she had been visiting with her Uncle Horace Shelby in the adjoining room.

"She had to get out of that room, lock the connecting door, get her clothes off, get on a nightie, get into bed, gulp down a few sleeping pills and then come staggering to the door and put on the act of being drugged so no one would suspect the real reason she didn't answer the door when we first knocked."

"That's a *wild* hunch," Della Street said.

Mason grinned. "Perhaps it is, but we're going back to Daphne's room, knock on the connecting door leading to the next room and sees what happens. And while I'm knocking on that door, Paul, you're going to be standing in the corridor so in case Uncle Horace tries to slip out, you'll be in a position to nab him. . . . Come on, let's go."

Chapter FOURTEEN

Mason went at once to the door at the side of Daphne Shelby's room, a door which apparently communicated with the adjoining room.

The lawyer tried the door. It was bolted.

He twisted the knurled knob so the bolt came open and quietly opened the door. Then he gently pressed against the door leading to the other room.

The door silently opened. The room was empty.

Mason hurriedly looked in the bathroom and the closet, and then ran to the hallway door and jerked it open.

Paul Drake was standing in the corridor.

"No one came out," Drake said.

"Quick!" Mason said. "He's smart. He checked out while we were in there with Daphne. She put on an act, not only to protect herself, but also to give him time for a getaway. Come on, let's go."

The lawyer raced down the corridor to the elevator, jabbed frantically on the button, and when the cage stopped, handed the operator a five-dollar bill, "All the way to the lobby, quick!" he said.

The cage doors clanged shut. The grinning operator dropped the cage to the lobby. Mason hurried to the cashier's desk.

"You had a check-out in 720?" he asked.

"Why, yes, just a few moments ago."

"What did the man look like?"

"Rather elderly, slender, distinguished-looking, but nervous—There he goes now!"

"Where?"

"Just through the revolving door to the street."

Mason raced across the lobby, out of the door, said to the doorman, "Get us a cab, quick!"

Again a five-dollar bill worked magic.

Mason, Della Street and Paul Drake jumped in the cab.

"Where to?" the cabby asked.

"Follow that man who's walking down the street," Mason said, "and don't let him know you're following. This is entirely legal but it's a ticklish matter. Here's twenty dollars to ease your conscience."

"Hell," the taxi driver said, "for twenty dollars I don't have any conscience to ease."

He pocketed the bill with a grin.

"That's in addition to the meter," Mason told him.

"Don't we want to stop him?" Drake asked.

"Hell, no," Mason said. "Let's see where he's going."

The man went to the hotel garage.

"He'll come out driving a car," Mason said to the cabdriver, "and we've got to follow him. . . . Paul, there's a telephone booth there. Get your office on the line, tell a couple of operatives to stick around. . . . How many cars do you have with telephones?"

"Two."

"Get them both in action," Mason said. "Start one east, one south."

Drake put through the calls.

It was a matter of nearly ten minutes before the man they were following emerged, driving a car with Massachusetts license plates.

Mason took one gleeful look at the license plates; then grabbed Drake by the arm. "That's Ralph Exeter's car."

Mason turned to the cabdriver. "You're going to have to follow him. It'll be difficult once he gets out of town, but do the best you can."

The cabdriver said, "I can beat him all to pieces in traffic, but if he gets out on the freeway and puts it into speed I'm going to have a hard time keeping up. These buses are geared down for city traffic, fast stops and starts, but not any great speed on the freeway."

"I know," Mason said, "do the best you can."

The elderly man drove the car cautiously, taking no chances, keeping well under the speed limits. The cab had no difficulty keeping up. The car ahead turned on the Santa Ana Freeway, began to gather speed.

The cabdriver had some difficulty keeping up, but the driver ahead kept in the outside right-hand lane and drove cautiously.

After ten minutes, the car stopped at a service station for gasoline.

"Need any gas?" Mason asked the cabdriver.

"I can use some."

"Pull in," Mason said.

"Isn't that dangerous?" Della Street asked.

"He doesn't know what *we* look like," Mason said.

The driver of the car with the Massachusetts license plates went to the restroom.

Mason approached the attendant, gave him a twenty-dollar bill, "We're in a hurry," he said. "Could you get us serviced before the other car?"

The attendant grinned. "I can stall around a bit on that other car."

"Do that," Mason said.

Paul Drake was at the telephone.

"Get the number of your cruising car that's headed south," Mason said. "He's probably on the freeway here somewhere. Tell him where we are; give him the time and tell him to try and pick us up."

The lawyer paced back and forth on the hard surface in an ecstasy of impatience.

At length, the driver emerged from the restroom, and Mason had a good look at the man's face. It was an aristocratic face, a high thin nose, a stubby gray mustache, high cheekbones, blue eyes.

The man kept looking back over his shoulder, his eyes darting around nervously. He seemed to pay almost no attention to the taxicab, and Mason kept in the background as much as possible.

Drake emerged from the phone booth and nodded. "The man is about five miles behind us," Drake said. "He should catch up with us by the time we leave here."

"Good work," Mason said. "Those car phones are well worth the price, Paul."

Drake said, "These taxicabs are so darned conspicuous, Perry. He'll get wise if *we* follow him."

"That's why we're going out first," Mason said. "He's committed himself to the freeway now. There's not much chance he'll turn off."

"If he does, we're licked," Drake said.

"That's okay," Mason said. "It's a chance we've got to take. In this business every once in a while you have to take a real chance."

The attendant nodded to Perry Mason. "You're all filled," he said.

Mason paid the bill, said to the cabdriver, "Straight on down the freeway and go slow. Let that other car pass us if it will."

"It's hard to recognize cars coming from behind," the driver said. "All headlights look alike."

"I know," Mason said, "we've got to wait until he passes us."

"Hold everything!" Drake exclaimed. "Here's my agency car!"

A big sleek, black sedan drove alongside. The driver tapped the horn a couple of times.

"Pull off to the side and stop." Mason said to the cabdriver. "Here's twenty dollars. That'll cover your fare out here and back. Let me have your number so I can get you as a witness if I want you."

"You're Perry Mason, the lawyer, aren't you?" the cabdriver asked.

"That's right."

"It'll be a pleasure to be a witness for you, Mr. Mason. Here's my card."

The cab came to a stop. The passengers jumped into the big sedan.

A few moments later, Drake, who had been looking out of the back window, said, "Here comes our man, Perry."

"How much gas you got?" Mason asked the driver of Drake's car.

Drake grinned. "Don't worry, Perry. He starts out with a full tank. Every one of these agency cars is filled to the brim whenever we park it."

Mason sighed with relief. "Okay," he said, "this should be easy."

The Massachusetts car drove on past. The agency car fell in behind.

"Jockey around a bit," Mason said. "Don't keep a fixed distance behind him."

Drake grinned, and said, "Practice law, Counselor, this man has forgotten more about shadowing than you'll ever know. It's a highly specialized profession and he can do it to perfection."

Mason settled back with a sigh. "I'm nervous as a cat," he admitted.

"I don't get all this," Drake said. "What's Horace Shelby doing driving Ralph Exeter's car, and why did Daphne have him put in the adjoining room and—"

"Hold the questions," Mason interrupted. "We're getting the answers."

Della Street said, "This is no life for a working girl. We're apt to be in Tucson by the time I have to open the office in the morning."

"More likely Ensenada," Mason said.

They settled back for a long job of following, but to their surprise the car ahead stopped at a motel at San Diego, and the driver rented a room under the name of H. R. Dawson.

Mason himself gave instructions to the operative.

"We'll get you relief just as soon as possible," he said. "We need two or three operatives on the job. You report to Drake's office by telephone. You're going to have to stick it out to put the finger on the subject, but we should have someone to help you within an hour."

"It's all right. I can take it all night if I can get a cup of coffee once in a while," the operative said. "And I keep some pills here to keep me awake if it gets too rough. I can take it."

"Keep in touch by phone," Mason said; then to Paul Drake, "Get on the phone. Have your San Diego branch send an operative."

Drake nodded, said to the operative, "Phone the office and get two more relief cars sent down."

"Preferably another car with telephone," Mason pointed out.

"The other one started out on the San Bernardino Freeway," Drake said. "I phoned the office to call him back. He can be down here by three o'clock in the morning."

"You'll get some immediate relief," Mason promised the driver. "Now, we've got to get a car and get back."

The driver used his phone to summon a taxicab. Mason had the cab take him to a car rental agency, and within half an hour the attorney, Della Street and Paul Drake were headed back north in the rented car.

"Do you know what this is all about?" Drake asked.

"Not for sure," Mason said. "But I'm beginning to have an idea."

"Don't we have to report what we've been doing?"

"Why?"

"If that's Horace Shelby, he's suspect in a murder case the minute he drives the car belonging to the murdered man."

"Suspect by whom?" Mason asked.

"The police."

"But not by me," Mason said. "Heaven forbid! *We* know that he wouldn't do anything like that!"

"How do you know?"

"Because Daphne herself said so. She said that Uncle Horace wouldn't harm a fly."

"Perhaps there's been a personality change," Drake said dryly. "— I just don't feel comfortable not advising the police that we've located the car of the murdered man."

"The police haven't asked us anything about it," Mason said. "We've got to give Horace Shelby a break."

"What kind of a break?"

"We're going to let him be his own man for a while and have a chance to recover his poise. We're also going to give him a chance to outwit the police just as much as possible. If his half brother tries to show that he's incompetent again, we can show that he was outwitting Lieutenant Tragg, and that calls for rather a high I.Q."

"I thought you were going to try and make him the murderer and prove that he was legally insane," Della Street said.

Mason grinned. "The good campaigner changes his battle plans in accordance with changing facts."

"And facts have changed?" they asked.

"Greatly," Mason said. "Now, here are some things we need to do, Paul.

"First get an operative to check into the Northern Lights Motel. You can phone in instructions from the next pay phone. Have him check in tonight."

"Why?"

"Because the place will be filled up," Mason said. "The only vacancy will be Unit 21. The police have removed the body, photographed the room, and by this time have released it for rental.

"If your man checks in now, he'll get Unit 21.

"Now then, have *another* man use his official I.D. card and go to the motel early in the morning. Have him ask to see the registration cards and have him get the numbers of all cars with Nevada license plates.

"Run down these registrations, if there are any, and run a preliminary check on the owners, who they are, what they do."

"Will do," Drake said. "How about letting me drive awhile? It's a long way home."

"Wait another half an hour," Mason said, "I'm jittery as a cat in a thunderstorm and I've got a lot of thinking to do."

"That," Della Street announced in a tone of finality to the detective, "is an invitation to us to keep quiet."

Chapter FIFTEEN

A rather exhausted Della Street entered the office at ten o'clock the next morning to find Perry Mason already on the job.

"Perry!" she exclaimed in surprise. "How long have *you* been here?"

"About half an hour," Mason said, grinning. "Get any sleep?"

"Just exactly half enough," Della Street said. "Man, how I hated to get up."

"Things are moving," Mason said. "Paul Drake's man from San Diego telephoned. Horace Shelby has crossed the border, gone through Tijuana and is on his way to Ensenada. Apparently, he doesn't have the faintest idea that anyone is following him, and he's breezing along as happy as a lark, driving faster and with more assurance. But he's no longer in the Massachusetts car."

"He isn't?"

"No, he parked that one in San Diego, purchased a used car for cash at one of the car lots which was open early in the morning."

"What about Daphne?"

Mason grew serious. "They don't have a thing in the world against her," he said, "but the district attorney's office has had a complete report from the police, has read a lot of unwarranted meaning into the evidence and wants to try her. They think they've got a case."

"What do you think?"

Mason closed his right eye in a wink, said, "I'm playing both ends against the middle, but I'm only representing Daphne, not anyone else. No matter what *she* wants me to do, I'm protecting *her* interests."

"What have you done?"

"Demanded a preliminary hearing," Mason said.

"Do they have enough evidence to bind her over?"

"They think so. They are absolutely convinced that Ralph Exeter was in the motel unit after Horace Shelby had left, that Daphne bought the Chinese food for him, and that Daphne and Exeter are the two who ate the food."

"In which case, she gave him the barbiturates?" Della Street asked. Mason nodded.

"How do they know Horace Shelby wasn't there?"

"They've found the taxi driver that Paul Drake uncovered."

"Do we have anything new?"

"Drake's man is already planted in Unit 21 at the motel."

"Any trouble?" she asked.

"None whatever. Now, Della, we've had some dealings with Bill Hadley, the physicist detective."

"The one who specializes in automobile accidents?"

Mason nodded. "He knows metallurgy and all that stuff and can tell how fast cars were going because of the degree of impact and all that. I just have an idea that he might take a look at that disconnected gas pipe and come up with some answers the police don't have as yet.

"They've accepted the gas pipe as just one of those things, but actually you don't disconnect a gas pipe with your fingers. It takes tools, and regardless of what the police may think at the present time, no jury is going to feel that a girl like Daphne would have been carrying a bunch of tools with her to disconnect gas pipes."

Della Street's face lit up. "Why, *that's* a thought," she said. "That had never occurred to me."

"I don't think it's occurred to Hamilton Burger, the district attorney," Mason said, grinning.

"Get Bill Hadley on the telephone."

A few moments later when Della Street had the physicist on the line, Mason said, "Bill, you've worked for me in a few automobile accident cases. This time I want you to work in a murder case. Get over to the Northern Lights Motel; get into Unit 21. A murder was committed there—at least the police think it was a murder. A gas pipe was disconnected and a man who had been put to sleep with barbiturates was asphyxiated."

"What do you want me to do?" Hadley asked.

"Find out what happened," Mason said.

"Am I supposed to be clairvoyant or something?"

Mason said, "Take a look at that gas pipe. You don't disconnect a gas pipe with fingers."

"Can I get in?" Hadley asked. "Do I have to show any authority or—"

"None whatever," Mason interrupted. "Go there as soon as possible. You'll find the occupant will be very courteous as soon as you identify yourself. The pipe has been reconnected. See what you can find out."

"I take it I am to bring cameras and take pictures?"

"Bring cameras, floodlights, microscopes, the works."

"Okay," Hadley said, "anything else?"

"Don't let anybody on the outside know what you're doing," Mason said. "The man in the unit is all right."

"Okay," Hadley told him, "I'll start getting things together right now. I'll be there early in the afternoon."

"Don't arouse suspicions," Mason warned.

"Shucks, I'll be a tourist from the country," Hadley promised, "a regular shutterbug."

Mason hung up, said to Della Street, "Now, I'm going down and see Daphne and see what kind of a night *she* had."

"The poor kid," Della Street said.

"Well, it depends upon how you look at it," Mason told her. "You have to admit she pulled a fast one getting her uncle to take that adjoining room and then pulling that sleep medicine gag."

"I suppose they'll use that against her," Della Street said.

"Oh, sure. Tragg fished every last pellet out of the stomach contents."

The lawyer chuckled. "I can't get over remembering the squawk she made when she hit that cold water in the bathtub, thinking it was going to be lukewarm."

Mason left the office, went to the detention ward and muttered expressions of sympathy as a bedraggled Daphne Shelby, who had quite evidently passed a sleepless night, was brought into the consulting room by the matron.

"Pretty rough, Daphne?" Mason asked.

She started to cry but then caught herself, threw her head back defiantly and said, "It's rough, but I can take it."

Mason said, "Somehow it seems impossible to impress upon you that you should play fair with your lawyer."

"What have I done now?"

"It's what you haven't done. You forgot to tell me about your Uncle Horace having been registered in the hotel in that room right next to yours—720—and the fact that you had been in there talking with him which was the reason you didn't hear me when I first knocked on the door of your room."

"Mr. Mason," she said, "let's have one understanding. I'm going to be fair and play fair with you except for one thing. I'm not going to tell you anything that might hurt Uncle Horace."

"You know by this time he isn't related to you?"

"I can't help it, I have a feeling for him. I've been like a daughter to him. I've watched over him and guarded him, and now he's an old man and he's sick and I'm going to protect him in every way that I can."

"Do the officers know anything about his being in the adjoining room?" Mason asked.

She shook her head. "I don't think so."

"Then you haven't told them?"

"Heavens, no!"

"Their questions haven't indicated that they have any idea he was there?"

"No."

"Did you know that he was driving Ralph Exeter's car?"

She looked him defiantly in the eyes, took a long breath, and said, "No!"

"All right," Mason said, "We're playing games, Daphne. You're playing games with me to protect your uncle. Now, *I'm* going to tell *you* something. I'm representing you. I'm going to try and get you acquitted on this murder charge.

"I'm not representing your uncle. I'm not representing anyone except you. I'm going to try every legal and ethical strategy that I know of to get you acquitted. That's my duty. Do you understand that?"

"Yes, I guess so."

"You're going to have to stay here for a while," Mason said.

"I'll get accustomed to it."

Mason got up to go.

Suddenly her hand was on his arm. "Please, Mr. Mason, I can take it. I'm young. I'm resilient. I can stand it; but if Uncle Horace got in one of these places, if he had bars over the windows and guards and cells and things of that sort, he'd go absolutely crazy."

Mason smiled down at her. "Daphne," he said, "I'm protecting you. A lawyer doesn't have room for more than one allegiance. You'll have to get accustomed to that."

"And," she said, "I'm protecting Uncle Horace. You'll have to get accustomed to *that*."

Mason grinned. "I've learned to accustom myself to that," he said, and then added, "the hard way."

Mason returned to his office to find that Paul Drake had a significant report. A Nevada car had been registered at the Northern Lights Motel. The owner had registered as Harvey Miles of Carson City, but the car was registered in the name of Stanley Freer of Las Vegas.

"Get a rundown?" Mason asked.

"On Freer, yes," Drake said. "Miles seems to be simply a name, but Freer is a collector."

"A collector?"

"Yes. They use him when some tinhorn tries to squirm out of paying a gambling debt."

"Methods?" Mason asked.

"Since gambling debts are illegal in most states," Drake said, "the methods used by Freer are reported to be illegal—but highly successful.

"Now, if Exeter owed a gambling debt and Freer called on him and perhaps told him Horace Shelby was hiding in Unit 21 at the Northern Lights, it's a cinch Exeter would have gone there to try a shakedown.

"At least that's the way I figure it."

Mason was thoughtfully silent. At length he said, "That figures,

Paul. Some men from Nevada were watching the sanitarium. They were anxious to talk with the doctor the Court appointed.

"That means the gamblers were getting tired of waiting, and it also means they were very much on the job.

"They could have discovered when Horace Shelby left the place and where he went. Then they told Exeter they weren't going to wait for Shelby to die, that it was up to Exeter to get the money *or else*.

"Then a 'collector' would have tagged along to see what Exeter was doing—and if Exeter bungled the job, the collector *might* have lowered the boom on him."

"It's a possibility," Drake agreed. "Those collectors are willing to write a debt off every once in a while in order to throw a scare into the pigeons. If word gets around a man who gets too delinquent in payments doesn't stay healthy, it helps with collections everywhere.

"Usually, however, they get some muscle men to give a guy a beating first."

Mason thought the situation over. "A jury might buy that theory, Paul. I might even buy it myself."

Chapter SIXTEEN

Marvin Mosher, one of the leading trial deputies of the district attorney's office, addressed Judge Linden Kyle, who had just taken the bench.

"May I make an opening statement, if the Court please?"

"It is not usual at a preliminary hearing," Judge Kyle said.

"I understand, Your Honor, but the purpose of a preliminary opening statement is so that the Court may understand the purpose of the testimony which is being elicited and co-ordinate that testimony into the whole picture."

"We have no objection," Mason said.

"Go ahead," Judge Kyle said, "but I suggest you be brief. A trial judge becomes rather adept at co-ordinating testimony."

"Very well," Mosher announced, "I will present the matter in a very brief summary.

"The defendant, Daphne Shelby, thought until a few days ago that she was the niece of Horace Shelby, a man of some seventy-five years of age.

"She had acted as this man's niece and, as the evidence will show, had ingratiated herself with him and was on the point of using that relationship to secure a very material financial advantage.

"It was at this point Shelby's half brother, Borden Finchley, and his wife, Elinor, accompanied by a friend, came to call on Horace Shelby. They were shocked at what they found, the extent to which this young woman had ingratiated herself and the extent to which Horace Shelby had become dependent upon her."

"Now, just a minute," Judge Kyle interrupted, "you say the defendant *thought* she was the niece of Horace Shelby?"

"That is correct, Your Honor. I am coming to that, if the Court will bear with me."

"Go right ahead. The Court is interested in this."

"The Finchleys suggested that the defendant take a three-month vacation, that they would take care of Horace Shelby while she was gone and take charge of the household affairs. The defendant was quite run-down, and, in fairness to her, we should state that she had been very solicitous in her care of the man with whom she was living as a niece, a very devoted niece.

"The defendant was given ample funds to take a trip to the Orient on shipboard. She was to be gone three months.

"While she was gone, the Finchleys learned not only that Horace Shelby intended to make her the sole beneficiary under his will, but that he had been giving the defendant large sums of money and was preparing to give her even larger sums of money."

"What do you mean, large sums of money?" Judge Kyle asked.

"The last amount, the one which triggered the action on the part of the Finchleys, was a check for one hundred and twenty-five thousand dollars."

"For *how* much?" Judge Kyle asked.

"A hundred and twenty-five thousand dollars."

"Was this woman his niece?"

"She was not, Your Honor. She was a complete stranger to the blood. She was the daughter of Horace Shelby's former housekeeper, a daughter by an affair which had taken place at the other end of the continent.

"I will state in the defendant's favor, however, that she, in good faith, thought Horace Shelby was her uncle. He had led her so to believe."

"And the mother?" Judge Kyle asked.

"Her mother had passed away a relatively short time ago. She had been Horace Shelby's housekeeper for some twenty years.

"The Finchleys found that Horace Shelby had deteriorated mentally, that he had exaggerated ideas as to what he considered his duty toward the defendant, that the defendant was carrying on a course which could well strip this rather elderly man of every cent he had in the world. And when the Finchleys found that Horace Shelby was giving this young woman a check for a hundred and twenty-five thousand dollars, they went to court and asked that a conservator be appointed."

"That is quite understandable," Judge Kyle said, looking curiously at Daphne.

"When Daphne returned from the Orient," Mosher went on, "and found that the fortune that she expected to inherit within a short time was being placed beyond her grasp, she became furious. Horace Shelby, at the time, had been placed in a sanitarium for treatment.

"Daphne Shelby secured employment in that institution, using an assumed name and taking a job as a domestic for just long enough to surreptitiously aid Horace Shelby in making an escape. She took him to a motel known as the Northern Lights Motel. She placed him in Unit 21.

"From that day on, if the Court please, none of the real relatives of Horace Shelby have seen him or heard from him. The police were and are unable to find him. Horace Shelby, with the connivance of this defendant, vanished into thin air *after making a will leaving everything to this defendant.* He may well be dead.

"Moreover, and by the use of an ingenious fraud perpetrated upon the Court, and despite the appointment of a conservator, the defendant managed to get her hands on fifty thousand dollars of Horace Shelby's funds.

"The decedent, Bosley Cameron, alias Ralph Exeter, was a friend of the Finchleys, and as such, familiar with the facts. It appears that in some way Exeter traced Horace Shelby to the Northern Lights Motel. The evidence will indicate that the defendant lured Exeter into the room occupied by Horace Shelby at a time shortly after Horace Shelby had left the place.

"The defendant went to a nearby Chinese restaurant, secured food in containers and, using the bottom of a glass toothbrush container as a pestle, and a tumbler in the motel as a mortar, ground up sleeping pills which had been given her to take on her trip in case she became unduly nervous.

"She placed this barbiturate in the food which was given Exeter, and after Exeter became unconscious, left him in the motel after first deliberately unscrewing the gas feed pipe which went to a vented heating appliance in the unit.

"Exeter's body was found when a neighboring tenant smelled gas. He was quite dead. Death had apparently been due to gas, but he had first been rendered unconscious by the barbiturate.

"This young woman then went to the Hollander-Heath Hotel, and when officers traced her there, hurriedly swallowed some barbiturates of the same brand as those which had been administered to Ralph Exeter, telling the officers a concocted story about how some chocolate she had taken had been poisoned.

"The obvious purpose of this was to lead the officers to believe that some third person had administered the poison to Ralph Exeter.

"Now, I would like to state to the Court that the reason this case is being prosecuted at this time is because of recent decisions of our higher courts aimed at protecting the innocent, but which unduly complicate the duties of a prosecutor and of the police.

"This young woman has refused to co-operate with us. She has refused to answer questions without her attorney being present. Her attorney has advised her to make no statement in regard to certain key matters, and, as a result, we are left with no alternative but to marshal the evidence that we have and present our case to the Court.

"We wish to call the Court's attention to a matter which is, of course, elemental. At this time we only need to show that a crime has been committed and to show reasonable grounds for believing that the defendant perpetrated the crime. In that event, the Court is duty bound to hold the defendant for trial in the higher court."

Mosher sat down.

Judge Kyle said, "If the proof bears out the statement, there is certainly no doubt that the Court should bind the defendant over for trial.

"This Court has frequently announced that some of the recent decisions protecting the rights of defendants sometimes boomerang and force the authorities to take official action, whereas if the authorities had more time for a detailed investigation such formal action might have been spared.

"However," and here Judge Kyle smiled, "this Court has no authority to overrule decisions of our higher tribunals. You may proceed with the case."

"May I make an opening statement?" Mason asked.

"Why, yes, if you desire," Judge Kyle said, "although this is entirely unusual."

Mason said, "The evidence will show that the Finchleys had for years taken no interest in Horace Shelby. When they learned, however, that Shelby had become comparatively wealthy, they came to visit him; and on finding that Shelby had made a will, or intended to make a will leaving his property to the defendant, they hustled the defendant off to the Orient and in the three months that they had Horace Shelby under their control, exasperated him to such a point that the man was desperate.

"Learning of their intentions to railroad him into a sanitarium, Shelby tried to get a substantial part of his fortune in the form of cash out from under the control of the Finchleys so that he would have some money with which to fight the case as he saw fit. He therefore asked the defendant to take charge of that money.

"She tried to do so, but was prevented by an order of the Court appointing a conservator.

"As to the fifty thousand dollars which the prosecutor would have the Court believe the defendant had secured by artifice and fraud, the money was secured legally and through my efforts. It was given to the defendant, and she, in turn, gave the bulk of that money to Horace Shelby so that he would be able to spend his own funds.

"We expect to show that Ralph Exeter was a professional gambler indebted to other gamblers; that the Finchleys were, in turn, indebted to him, and that Exeter was the driving force behind this situation, suggesting to the Finchleys that they use their connection and relationship to Horace Shelby to raise immediate money.

"We expect to show, at least by circumstantial evidence, that Ralph Exeter found where Horace Shelby was located; that Exeter made demands upon him, offering to let Shelby keep his liberty in return for a substantial cash payment.

"We expect to show that Shelby mashed up some sleeping pills which had been given him by the defendant, put them in food which was given Exeter for the sole purpose of enabling Shelby to escape from the clutches of his oversolicitous relatives.

"It is our contention that after the defendant had left the motel; after the departure of Horace Shelby, while Ralph Exeter was asleep in the room, someone disconnected the gas pipe and asphyxiated Exeter."

"You can prove this?" Judge Kyle asked.

"We can prove it," Mason said.

Judge Kyle was thoughtful for a few moments, then said to Mosher, "Very well, put on your proof."

Mosher called witness after witness, building an iron-clad case of circumstantial evidence.

Dr. Tillman Baxter identified Daphne; told of how she had applied for a job; how she had enabled Horace Shelby to escape.

He described Shelby's condition in technical terms. He was, he explained, suffering from the first definite stage of senile dementia; that the Court had appointed a doctor, Dr. Grantland Alma, to examine Horace Shelby; that that examination was to have taken place on the afternoon of the day when Shelby had been spirited from his institution.

Dr. Baxter said he had been looking forward to having his diagnosis confirmed by an independent psychiatrist, but that the action of the defendant in enabling Horace Shelby to escape had foreclosed any opportunity to learn of the man's actual condition.

Lieutenant Tragg told of finding Ralph Exeter, also known as Bosley Cameron, dead in the motel unit at the Northern Lights. He had found in the room a glass tumbler. In the glass tumbler was the glass container in which new toothbrushes are sold. This had been used as a pestle in grinding up pills which were identified as sleeping pills of a trade name known as Somniferone; that these were the same pills which were subsequently taken by the defendant in the hotel at a time when her attorney visited her, apparently to warn her of the impending visit of the officers.

Lieutenant Tragg gleefully described the manner in which the malingering of the defendant had been exposed by her own attorney, who was putting her in what she thought was a tub of lukewarm water but was actually ice cold.

Tragg was temporarily withdrawn. A clerk in a drugstore near the Northern Lights Motel identified the glass toothbrush container as being similar to the container in which a toothbrush of a certain standard brand was marketed. He identified the defendant as having stopped in his store earlier that day and purchasing a toothbrush and toothpaste, a hairbrush and comb, a safety razor and shaving cream, and a small plastic bag in which they could be carried. She had explained that her uncle had lost all of his baggage and needed these articles immediately.

The waitress at the Chinese restaurant identified Daphne as being the person who had purchased Chinese food in containers to take out, explaining that she was getting the food for her uncle who was very fond of Chinese food.

The waitress described the manner in which Daphne had waited while the food was being prepared. She was, the waitress said, exceedingly nervous.

Mason listened to these witnesses with a detached air of idle curiosity, as though their testimony not only related to some matter in which he had no interest, but that the testimony itself was immaterial. He didn't bother to cross-examine any of the witnesses until Lieutenant Tragg had returned to the stand and finished his testimony. Then Mason arose and smiled affably at the police officer.

"You say the pipe which connected the gas heater to the gas supply had been unscrewed, Lieutenant?"

"Yes."

"And you gave it as your conclusion that this had been done after the decedent had become unconscious from the barbiturates?"

"As an investigating officer, I felt that was a reasonable interpretation," Lieutenant Tragg said. "The autopsy bears this out with indisputable proof.

"I took into consideration that the unscrewing of such a pipe would be accompanied by considerable noise, and Exeter could hardly have been expected to sit idly by while the preparations for his death were being carried out."

"Unless, of course, he had committed suicide," Mason said.

Lieutenant Tragg smiled a triumphant smile. "If he committed suicide, Mr. Mason, he disposed of the weapon, and when we find a missing weapon we usually discount the theory of suicide."

"Weapon?" Mason asked.

"A small pipe wrench," Lieutenant Tragg said. "The gas pipe had been joined to the heater so that there would be no leak, and it took a pipe wrench to loosen a three-inch section of the connecting pipe. There was no wrench in the room."

"Ah, yes," Mason said, affably, "I was coming to that, Lieutenant. You've anticipated the point I was going to make. It took a pipe wrench to loosen the gas feed line?"

"Yes, indeed."

"In order to prevent leaks, these lines are customarily screwed up very tight?"

"Yes, sir."

"Sometimes with a compound which furnishes a seal and prevents leakage?"

"That's right."

"And in order to loosen this pipeline, it took considerable force, did it not?"

Tragg avoided the trap. "Quite a bit of force," he admitted, "but nothing that a reasonably strong young woman in good health couldn't have done, if that's what you're getting at."

"That's not what I'm getting at, Lieutenant," Mason said. "The point is that a pipe wrench has to bite into the pipe in order to get a firm enough hold in order to unscrew the pipe."

"That's right."

"Now, these pipe wrenches have jaws with sharp ridges on them so that when pressure is applied to the handle the jaws tighten and the corrugations or ridges on the jaw bite into the pipe enough to keep the pipe from slipping. Is that right?"

"Yes, sir."

"And it is because you found indentations in this pipe that you knew it had been loosened with a pipe wrench?"

"Yes, sir."

"Now then, did you photograph these marks on the pipe, Lieutenant?"

"Photograph them?"

"That's right."

"No, sir, why should I have photographed them?"

"Did you then disconnect the pipe so that it could be used as evidence?"

"Certainly not. Gas was escaping. We reconnected the pipe just as promptly as possible."

"But you did notice these marks on the pipe?"

"Yes, sir."

"Didn't it occur to you, Lieutenant, that those marks which were on the pipe might be very significant?"

"Certainly, it did. They were significant in that they showed a pipe wrench had been used, and that's the extent of their significance."

"Did you," Mason asked, "examine those marks under a microscope?"

"I did not."

"Under a magnifying glass?"

"No, sir."

"You knew, did you not, Lieutenant, that in the case of chisels or knives being used on wood it quite frequently happens that some blemish in the blade leaves an imprint in the wood so that the instrument used can be identified?"

"Certainly, anyone knows that."

"But did you also realize, Lieutenant, that on some of these pipe wrenches one of the ridges on the jaws becomes damaged or nicked so that that wrench leaves an indelible identifying mark upon any pipe on which it may be used?"

Lieutenant Tragg's face showed that he suddenly realized the point that Mason was making and its significance.

"We didn't remove the pipe," he admitted. "It's still there in its original condition."

"It has, however, been screwed back into the appliance?"

"Yes, sir."

"And as of this date, Lieutenant, you don't know whether there were any distinctive markings in the indentations on that pipe which would give an indication of the wrench that had been used in unscrewing it?"

Lieutenant Tragg shifted his position, then finally said, "I will admit, Mr. Mason, that you have a point there. I don't know. I will also admit that perhaps the better practice would have been to have examined those markings carefully under a microscope. I have always tried to be fair. The investigation of a crime is frequently a scientific matter. I will admit in this case it would have been better practice to have examined those indentations with a magnifying glass, and in the event any distinctive marks had been found, to have photographed them."

"Thank you very much for a very impartial statement, Lieutenant

Tragg. I have always appreciated your integrity, and I now appreciate your fairness. I have no further questions."

Judge Kyle said, "Well, gentlemen, it seems we have covered a lot of ground today. I assume that the case can be finished in a few hours tomorrow?"

"I would think so," the deputy district attorney said.

"Very well," Judge Kyle said, "it's the hour of the evening adjournment and Court will adjourn until tomorrow morning at nine-thirty o'clock. The defendant is remanded. Court's adjourned."

Chapter SEVENTEEN

Back in his office, Mason found Paul Drake with a supplemental report on Horace Shelby.

"The guy's doing pretty good," Drake said. "He's down there in Ensenada soaking up sunlight, walking around with a lot more assurance than when he first arrived, and he seems to be enjoying himself."

"Anybody talk with him yet?" Mason asked.

"Not as an interview. But one of my men managed to engage him in conversation when Shelby was taking a stroll down on the wharf, and he reports the man is bright as a dollar."

Mason sighed. "All right, I guess he can stand another shock by this time."

"You going down?"

"I'm going down," Mason said. "I'll have 'Pinky' fly me by fast twin-motored plane to San Diego, then pick up Francisco Munoz at Tijuana and— Instruct your man to be looking for me. I'll meet him in front of the motel."

"Will do," Drake said.

"Now then," Mason said, "I want to be sure that you don't lose either Borden Finchley or his wife tonight. I want a shadow on them every minute of the time. Put on two or three operatives with cars if you have to."

"I've already got them," Drake said.

"What are the Finchleys doing?"

"Living normally. They went up to court to hear the evidence and then they went back home."

"Watch them carefully," Mason said. "Della and I are going to Ensenada. Come on, Della."

"No dinner?" Della asked.

Mason said, "A wonderful dinner. Genuine turtle soup, fried quail, a little venison steak on the side, if you'd care for it, some Santo Tomas wine and—"

"You mean we're eating in Mexico?"

"I mean we're eating in Mexico," Mason said. "Ring up Pinky and Francisco Munoz and let's go. The sooner we get started, the sooner we eat."

Della Street sighed. "A girl can't keep on a diet in Ensenada. It would be a crime to order a cottage cheese salad under such circumstances."

Her fingers started flying over the telephone dial.

Mason turned back to Paul Drake.

"Now then, Paul," he said, "do you know anything about the technique of taking a pipe wrench, putting a piece of chamois skin around the jaws so that you can get a tight enough grip on a bit of metal so you can unscrew it but so the jaws don't leave any mark in the metal?"

"I've seen it done," Drake said.

Mason handed Paul Drake a section of pipe.

"Have your man at the Northern Lights get the section of pipe which connects the gas feed to that heating stove out of there and replace it with this pipe."

Paul Drake took the piece of pipe which Mason handed him.

"Will this fit?" he asked.

"This will fit," Mason said. "Very careful measurements have been taken."

Drake turned the piece of pipe over slowly in his hands. "This has deep marks on it," he said, "the marks of a pipe wrench and—there's a nick in one of the jaws?"

"Exactly," Mason said.

"Now, look here," Drake said, "this is substituting evidence."

"Evidence of what?"

"You know what I mean. Evidence of murder. At least, evidence in a homicide case."

Mason said, "Carefully remove the piece of pipe that's now in there and be careful you don't leave any marks on it. Use chamois skin to enable you to get a grip on the pipe without leaving any marks from your pipe wrench or obliterating any marks now on it. Take that piece of pipe into custody and hold it until Tragg asks you for it."

"It's still concealing evidence."

"Concealing evidence, my eye," Mason said. "You're taking the evidence into your custody. It's evidence that Tragg didn't want. Now, get busy and get this thing done fast before somebody raises a question about it."

Drake sighed. "You can skate faster and on thinner ice than anybody I ever worked with."

"You'll get a man on the job right away?"

Drake nodded.

"It has to be right away," Mason said. "A lot may depend on it. I want it done within an hour, while Tragg is reporting what happened in court."

Della said, "Pinky will have the plane waiting for us, all gassed up and ready to go."

"Let's go," Mason said.

"We'll be back tonight?" Della Street asked.

"We'll be back tonight," Mason said, "and in court in the morning."

Chapter EIGHTEEN

The taxicab came to a stop at Casa de Mañana Motel.

Mason assisted Della Street from the cab, paid off the driver.

"No wait?" the driver asked.

"No wait," Mason said, smiling. "Thank you very much. *Gracias!*"

The driver thanked Mason for the tip, started the car and drove on.

Mason and Della Street stood where he had left them.

Inskip, Paul's detective, gave a low whistle from a parked car, and Mason and Della Street crossed over to that car.

"Unit five," Inskip said. "He's in there."

The lawyer said, "Wait here, Inskip, you'll be taking us to the airport and then your job will be over."

The lawyer and Della Street walked under some banana trees, past the office down a wide corridor, and Mason knocked on the door of Number 5.

There was no answer; no sound of stirring within.

Mason knocked again.

The door opened a tentative crack.

Mason surveyed the anxious face, smiled reassuringly and said,

"I'm Perry Mason, Mr. Shelby, and this is my secretary, Della Street. We thought it was time to have a talk with you."

"You . . . *you're* . . . Perry Mason?"

"That's right."

"How did you—Oh, well, never mind, come in."

Shelby opened the door.

"I was getting ready to retire for the night," he explained apologetically, putting on his coat.

Mason patted him reassuringly on the shoulder, walked over and sat down on the edge of the bed. Della Street seated herself in one of the heavy leather chairs, and Horace Shelby took the other chair.

"It's been a long, hard battle for you," Mason said.

Shelby nodded. "You're the attorney representing Daphne."

"Yes."

"That poor kid."

"She's having troubles," Mason said.

Shelby looked up. "*She's* having troubles?"

"That's right."

"Why? She shouldn't be having any trouble!"

"I know she shouldn't."

"What sort of troubles?" Shelby asked.

"She's being tried for the murder of Ralph Exeter," Mason said, and stopped talking.

Shelby's face showed a succession of expressions—surprise, consternation, anger.

"You said murder?"

"I said murder."

"Ralph Exeter," Shelby said, spitting out the words. "A cheap, blackmailing, gambling fourflusher—so he's dead!"

"He's dead."

"You say it's murder?"

"Yes."

"Who killed him?"

"The police say Daphne did."

"She couldn't have."

"The police think she did."

"Where was he killed?"

"In Unit 21 at the Northern Lights Motel."

Shelby was silent for a long thoughtful period.

Della Street surreptitiously extracted her shorthand notebook from her purse and started taking notes.

Shelby said, at length, "Well, I guess I'd better face the music."

"The music?" Mason asked.

"If he was found dead in the room I occupied at the Northern Lights Motel, I killed him."

"How?" Mason asked.

"I gave him an overdose of sleeping pills," Shelby readily admitted.

"Suppose you tell me about it?" Mason asked.

"There's not much to tell. I have been through hell, Mr. Mason, absolute hell. I don't even want to think about it, much less to describe it."

"I know something of what you went through," Mason said.

"No, you don't. You see my experience from the light of a robust man in full possession of his faculties.

"I'm not a young man any more. I know that my mind wanders at times. There are times when I'm all right, and there are times when I feel—well, I feel sort of half asleep. I don't co-ordinate the way I should. I go to sleep when people are talking. I am not young.

"On the other hand, I'm not old. I'm able to take care of myself. I know what I want to do with my money. I know how I want to handle my business. You have no idea what it means to suddenly have the rug jerked out from under you; to be left without a five-cent piece in your pocket, not a dime that you can put your hand on that belongs to you; to have others telling you what to do; to have people giving you hypodermics, strapping you down in a bed.

"I wouldn't go through that again if I had to commit a dozen murders."

Mason nodded sympathetically.

"Daphne got me out of it," Shelby said, "bless her soul. She used her head. She got me down at that room in the Northern Lights."

"And then what?"

"She told me to stay under cover; that she'd come and bring me food."

"And she did?"

"Yes, she went to a Chinese restaurant and brought in some Chinese food."

"Then what?"

"After she left," Shelby said, "—and she hadn't been gone over two minutes, there was a knock at the door.

"I sat tight for a while, but the knock was repeated and I didn't want to attract attention to the unit by not answering the door. So I went to the door and opened it, and there was Ralph Exeter, smiling that nasty, oily smile of his and he said, 'I'm coming in, Horace,' and pushed his shoulder against the door and literally pushed his way into the room."

"Tell me what happened," Mason said. "I want to know about Ralph Exeter. Just what happened?"

"Exeter pushed his way into the room and put it right up to me," Shelby said. "He said that he was the one who controlled my future; that if I wanted to pay him a hundred and twenty-five thousand dollars I could go my way; that he'd see that Borden Finchley and his wife cleared out; that I could have what was left of my own money to do what I wanted to do with it; that if I didn't play ball with him he was going to turn me in to the authorities; that he was going to swear I was completely incompetent and that I'd spend the rest of my days in a sanitarium under the influence of dope or strapped to a cot."

"Go on," Mason said.

"You don't know what I'd been through, Mr. Mason. If it hadn't been for that experience, I'd have laughed at him and gone to the telephone and called the police. But the way it was, no one would have taken my word for anything. I'd have been considered crazy. I was desperate."

"What did you do?"

"Daphne had given me some sleeping pills to take in case I needed them. I stepped into the bathroom, ground up some of those sleeping pills in a glass, and came back into the room. I was going to try to slip them into a drink or something.

"But the guy played right into my hands. When I came back he was looking around at that Chinese food. He asked me, 'You got a plate and anything to eat this with?'

"I told him we had some chopsticks; that this food had been left over from stuff I'd been eating. He wanted the chopsticks. So I got them, and as I handed them to him, took the opportunity to dump the ground-up sleeping pills into the food.

"He cleaned it up.

"I told him that I'd have to try and figure things out a bit; that I'd agree with him on principle, but getting a hundred and twenty-five thousand in cash would wipe out my cash reserves. I told him I'd have to do some figuring.

"The sleeping pills began to take effect. It wasn't long before he stretched out on the bed, yawned, and went to sleep."

"And what did you do?"

"I washed the containers, took his car, went to the Hollander-Heath Hotel and managed to get the room next to Daphne's."

"Why did you take his car?" Mason asked.

"I had to," Shelby said. "I'd tried calling a taxicab earlier in the day. I had to go out and stand on the street corner to wait for it. That was dangerous."

"What did you do with the taxicab?"

"I went uptown and— Well, first I was going to the Union Station; then I decided to go to the airport. I had money and I wanted to rent an automobile.

"I got to the airport and tried to rent a car and neither one of the places there would let me have one unless I had my driver's license."

"You didn't have your driver's license?"

"I didn't have anything. I had a toothbrush, some pajamas, a hairbrush and comb, only the few little things that Daphne had bought for me."

"So what did you do?"

"I took a bus back to El Mirar and walked four blocks back to the motel."

"Go on," Mason said. "What happened after you got to the Hollander-Heath Hotel?"

"Daphne was in the room with me. She didn't hear people pounding on the door. She had a *Do Not Disturb* sign on her room, but she'd made the mistake of bolting the door from the inside, and that way people knew she was in there. She had to do something quick. She gulped the rest of the sleeping pills I had, jumped out of her clothes, put on a nightie and climbed into bed. Then she got up to open the door. She was going to put on an act until the sleeping pills began to take effect. She said they'd pump her stomach out and that this would mix things up enough so I'd have a chance to escape."

"Then what did you do?"

"She went through her end of it. I had to wait for a while to get just the right opportunity. I put the things she'd bought for me in that little plastic bag, went down to the desk, checked out; went over and got Ralph Exeter's car out of the garage, drove down to San Diego, parked the car, spent the night in a motel, went to a used car lot where they weren't so darned particular about my driving license and got a used car.

"I wanted to go farther down in Mexico, but this is as far as I could go without a tourist permit, and I couldn't get a tourist permit without proving citizenship and showing a driving license and all that sort of stuff."

"Is it true," Meson asked, "that Daphne is the daughter of your housekeeper?"

Shelby looked him square in the eyes. "It's true," he said, "and it's also true that I'm her father."

"What!" Mason exclaimed.

"That's the truth," Shelby said. "I wanted to marry Daphne's mother, but she hadn't been divorced and she couldn't get a divorce. Then my other brother and his wife got killed in an auto accident, and I felt we could bring Daphne up as my niece.

"But of course Borden Finchley would know that wasn't the truth, so I told Borden Finchley that Daphne was the daughter of my housekeeper and that the housekeeper had been pregnant when she came from the East to work for me.

"Borden Finchley never cared anything about me. I never let him know that I'd put by a goodly bit of money. I guess Ralph Exeter was the one who found out that I was fairly well-heeled.

"Borden was indebted to Ralph Exeter on a big gambling debt. Exeter was putting the screws on him. They came down to make a visit.

"The first time Borden and his wife had visited me in twenty-odd years. Then they got this devilish idea of getting rid of Daphne and started irritating me until I went off my rocker.

"You've no idea the things they did, the little things. And then they started giving me dope and the first thing I knew I was all mixed up. . . . Well, I've got over that now, I'm my own man. I'm going back and face the music. If I gave Ralph Exeter too much drug and he died, why that's a responsibility I've got to take. But all I was trying to do was to get him to go to sleep so I could get out of there, and that's the truth."

Mason said, "The sleeping pills didn't kill him. Somebody unscrewed the gas pipe and he was asphyxiated by gas."

"What!" Shelby exclaimed.

Mason nodded.

Shelby paused for a moment, then sighed, "Well, I guess I've got to take the rap," he said. "No one's ever going to believe it the other way."

"The police found out that you took a cab from the motel earlier. They knew that Daphne bought Chinese food for someone, and they thought that it must have been Ralph Exeter because they learned that you had left earlier."

"I left and then I came back," Shelby explained. "And when I did that I broke my promise to Daphne. She wanted me to stay right there, but I just wanted to have the means of escape and I wanted to have a car so I could go places."

Mason looked at his watch. "I have planes waiting," he said.

Horace Shelby sighed, took a new suitcase from under the bed, started packing clothes.

"Okay," he said, "it'll take me ten minutes to be ready."

Chapter NINETEEN

Court reconvened at nine-thirty. Judge Kyle said, "People versus Daphne Shelby."

Marvin Mosher was on his feet. "If the Court please," he said, "I wish to recall Lieutenant Tragg for further direct examination."

"Very well," Judge Kyle said, "Mr. Mason will forego any further cross-examination until you have finished your questions on direct examination."

Lieutenant Tragg returned to the stand.

Mosher said, "There was some question yesterday about the evidence of tool marks on the pipe in the motel. You stated that you had not taken that pipe as evidence. I will ask you, Lieutenant, if there has been any change in the situation since yesterday."

"Yes, sir."

"What is the present situation?"

"I went to that unit in the motel this morning and removed the section of the connecting pipe. I have it here."

Lieutenant Tragg handed the deputy prosecutor a section of pipe.

"We object, if the Court please," Mason said, "on the ground that no proper foundation has been laid."

"Just what do you mean by that, Mr. Mason?" the judge asked. "It was, I believe, your suggestion that because the police had *not* removed this pipe, they had not preserved the evidence."

"That is true." Mason said, "but the police can't prove that this is *now* the same pipe that was in the unit at the time they discovered the body."

"Oh, I think that's a technicality," Judge Kyle said. He turned to Lieutenant Tragg. "Was there any evidence that the pipe had been tampered with from the time you first saw it until you secured this section of pipe, Lieutenant?"

"None whatever."

"Were the tool marks which appear on this pipe the same as the ones which were on the pipe when you first saw it?"

"They seem to be entirely similar."

"Very well, I'll admit the pipe in evidence," Judge Kyle said.

"Cross-examine," Mosher snapped to Mason.

Mason arose and approached Lieutenant Tragg. "Have you," he asked, "examined these tool marks on the pipe through a magnifying glass?"

"No, sir, I haven't. I just secured the evidence before coming to court. I thought if you wanted it, we'd have it."

Lieutenant Tragg's smile was almost a smirk.

Mason produced a magnifying glass from his pocket, studied the tool marks on the pipe, handed the glass and the pipe back to Lieutenant Tragg.

"I invite you to study the tool marks now," he said. "Study them carefully."

Lieutenant Tragg adjusted the magnifying glass, rotated the pipe in his hand. Suddenly he seemed to stiffen.

"See anything?" Mason asked.

"I believe," Lieutenant Tragg said cautiously, "that there *is* evidence here that one of the tool marks is distinctive. One of the sharp edges on the jaws of the pipe wrench seems to have a flaw in it, a break."

"So that the tool with which this pipe was disconnected can be identified?"

"Possibly so," Lieutenant Tragg said.

"Then you admit that you overlooked a material piece of evidence?"

Tragg fidgeted uneasily, said, "Well, the evidence is now before the Court."

"Thank you," Mason said. "That's all."

"That concludes our case," Mosher said.

"Is there any defense?" Judge Kyle asked. "It would certainly seem that there is at least a *prima facie* case against this defendant."

"There will be a defense," Mason said. "And I call as my first witness, Horace Shelby."

"What!" Mosher exclaimed.

"My first witness will be Horace Shelby," Mason repeated.

"If the Court please, this comes as a very great surprise to the prosecution," Mosher said. "May I ask a fifteen-minute recess? I would like to report to the district attorney, personally."

"I will give you fifteen minutes," Judge Kyle said. "The case seems to be taking an unexpected turn."

When the judge had left the bench, Mason turned to Daphne.

"Daphne," he said, "you're going to have to prepare yourself for a shock. I don't want to tell you anything that's coming. I want it to be a surprise to you. They're going to be watching your reactions. I want them to see your surprise."

"You actually have Uncle Horace where you can call him as a witness?" she asked.

Mason nodded.

"Oh, don't do that!"

"Why not?"

"Because they'll take him and put him back in the sanitarium. They'll—"

"You must think I'm an amateur, Daphne," Mason interrupted. "I've had three expert psychiatrists examine your uncle—one of them late last night, two of them this morning. Your uncle has had a good night's sleep. He feels fine. He's been pronounced absolutely sane and bright as a new silver dollar. You've no idea how *that* makes him feel.

"These doctors are experts. They're the tops in their profession. The most that Borden Finchley could use to support his contentions was the testimony of general practitioners and this man who runs the rest home or so-called sanitarium. The men who say your uncle is normal are experts."

"Oh, I'm *so* glad, so terribly glad!"

"You like him, don't you?"

"I don't know why, Mr. Mason, but I just respect and admire that man so much."

"Well," the lawyer said, "we'll wait a few minutes and I think things will start working out for the better.

"You sit here, Daphne, and don't talk with anybody. I'll be back in a moment."

Mason sauntered over to the place where Paul Drake was waiting. "Got your men shadowing all the subjects, Paul?"

Drake nodded.

Mason stretched, yawned.

"You must know what you're doing," Drake said.

Mason laughed. "Do I look confident, Paul?"

"You look as though you were holding four aces."

"That's fine," Mason said. "Actually, all I have is a pair of deuces, and I'm shoving a stack of blues into the middle of the table."

Drake said, "Somehow I have an idea you're going to get away with it, too!"

"Let's hope," Mason said.

Suddenly Hamilton Burger, the district attorney, came striding into the courtroom, and Mosher promptly collared him for a conference.

"See what I mean?" Mason said. "They've telephoned the big boy himself to come down and see what this is all about."

Judge Kyle returned from chambers, took the bench, called court to order and said, "I see the district attorney himself is here in court. You are interested in this case, Mr. Burger?"

"Very much so, Your Honor. I'm going to watch developments with the greatest interest."

"May I ask why?"

"Because, Hamilton Burger said, "in the event the defendant did not murder Ralph Exeter, Horace Shelby did; and I want to see that every bit of legal procedure is handled in such a manner that we can't be jockeyed into a position of not being able to prosecute Horace Shelby."

"Very well," Judge Kyle said. "Proceed, Mr. Mason."

"Call Horace Shelby to the stand," Mason said.

Shelby took the oath and took his position on the witness stand, after smiling reassuringly at Daphne.

"Now, just a moment," Hamilton Burger said. "First, Your Honor, I want this witness warned that he is suspect in a murder case, either acting alone or as an accessory with the defendant, Daphne Shelby. I want him warned that anything he may say may be used against him at a later date."

Mason, on his feet, said, "Your Honor, I object to this as a flagrant contempt of Court; as an attempt to brow-beat a defense witness and frighten him so that he cannot give testimony."

"Furthermore," Hamilton Burger interjected, "I object to this witness giving testimony, on the ground that he is incompetent to testify; that he is suffering from a disease known as senile dementia."

Mason smiled and said, "I would like to have the district attorney make up his mind if he is certain the witness is incompetent to understand what he is doing. If that is the case, it would appear that having the Court instruct him that anything he might say could be used against him at a later date would be an empty act."

Judge Kyle smiled, then turned to the witness.

"The Court wants to ask you a few questions, Mr. Shelby."

"Yes, sir," Horace Shelby said.

"You understand that this is a courtroom?"

"Yes, sir."

"Then why are you here?"

"I'm called as a witness by the defense."

"You have been declared an incompetent by a Court in this county?"

"I don't know as to that. I was beset by greedy relatives who gave me drugs that I knew nothing about, who railroaded me into a so-called sanitarium where I was restrained against my will and strapped to a bed. I understand the Court that committed me has designated a doctor to examine me."

Mason was on his feet, "If the Court please," he said, "Dr. Grantland Alma, who was appointed by the Court to examine this man, has examined him and pronounces him absolutely competent, completely sane. Two other well-known psychiatrists have also examined him and pronounced him sane, as well as completely competent to conduct his own affairs. I can call these doctors if the Court wishes."

Judge Kyle smiled. "Does the district attorney continue to urge his point?"

Hamilton Burger held a whispered conference with Marvin Mosher, then said, "I understand, if the Court please, there are two doctors who will testify that he is suffering from senile dementia."

"Two general practitioners who could never qualify as specialists," Mason said. "The Court-appointed doctor pronounces him sane, and two outstanding psychiatrists also pronounce him sane and competent. If you wish to take up the Court's time having two general practitioners testify against three specialists, we can do so."

Hamilton Burger had another whispered conference, then said, "We will temporarily withdraw our objection, Your Honor, but we wish this witness warned."

Judge Kyle turned to the witness. "Mr. Shelby, the Court does not wish you to be intimidated in any way. The Court does, however, warn you that in accordance with a statement made by the district attorney of this county, you may be considered an accomplice, an accessory or a principal in connection with the crime with which this defendant is being charged. The Court, therefore, warns you that anything you may say may be used against you at a later date; that you are entitled to your own individual counsel at any stage of the proceedings.

"Now then, does Mr. Mason represent you as attorney?"

"Only to the extent of proving that I am sane and competent."

"He does not represent you in connection with possible charges which may be filed against you in connection with the death of Ralph Exeter?"

"No, sir."

"Do you wish to have an independent counsel advise you at this time as to your rights, duties and privileges in connection with that crime?"

"No, sir."

"Do you wish to go ahead and testify of your own free will?"

"Yes, sir."

"You understand the nature of the proceedings?"

"Yes, sir."

"You will keep in mind the admonition of the Court that anything you say may be used against you at a later date?"

"Yes, sir."

"Do you understand you do not have to answer any question where the answer may tend to incriminate you?"

"Yes, sir."

"Very well," Judge Kyle said, "proceed with your examination, Mr. Mason."

"Is the defendant related to you in any way, Mr. Shelby?" Mason asked.

Shelby looked straight ahead, said, "Yes, sir. She is my daughter."

"Your daughter?" Mason asked. "Speak up, please, so the Court can hear you."

There was a ripple of whispering in the audience in the back of the court. Judge Kyle frowned the spectators to silence.

"Will you explain, please?" Mason asked.

"The defendant is the daughter of the woman who was my house-keeper, a woman I loved deeply. I was prevented from marrying her because of legal complications, and afterwards it was deemed better to continue our relationship as it was with the understanding that Daphne would consider herself my niece.

"In order to protect her, I made a will. That will, of course, left everything to Daphne's mother. After Daphne's mother died, I intended to change the will to leave everything to Daphne, but it was one of those things I just never got around to doing until . . . until it was almost too late."

"You have made such a will now."

"Yes."

"It was made freely and of your own volition?"

"Yes."

"You were confined at the Goodwill Sanitarium?"

"Yes, sir."

"Voluntarily or against your will?"

"Very much against my will."

"What happened?"

"Daphne rescued me."

"And then what happened?"

Daphne, by this time, was sobbing quietly into her handkerchief. There was a silence throughout the courtroom which was almost tangible.

Horace Shelby went on to tell his story, describing in detail his escape from the sanitarium, his tenancy at the Northern Lights Motel, the demands of Ralph Exeter, the manner in which he had drugged him, the stealing of his car.

Spectators sat forward on the edge of their chairs to listen. Hamilton Burger, from time to time, conferred with his deputy in worried whispers.

At length, Mason turned to the prosecution's table. "Do you wish to cross-examine?" he asked.

Hamilton Burger said, "If the Court please, this testimony has taken us completely by surprise. It is almost noon and we ask that the Court give us until two o'clock this afternoon to plan our strategy."

"Very well," Judge Kyle said, "the Court will take a recess until two o'clock this afternoon."

Judge Kyle left the bench.

Horace Shelby hurried to Daphne, embraced her.

Daphne was laughing and crying.

Newspaper reporters who had been alerted to the dramatic developments in the courtroom hurried to telephones.

Paul Drake came up to Perry Mason.

"Something funny, Perry," he said in a low voice.

"What?"

"At the recess this morning after Lieutenant Tragg gave his testimony, Borden Finchley went down to the place where his car was parked. He got into the car, drove out to a vacant lot pretty well covered with weeds, looked up and down the street to see if anyone was interested in what he was doing, took a wrench from his car, went into the vacant lots, fooled around a little while and then dropped the wrench."

"Your man was shadowing him?"

"Yes."

"Did your man get the wrench?"

"Not yet. He didn't have an opportunity. He continued to shadow Borden Finchley."

"And what did Finchley do?"

"Got in his car and drove back to the courthouse to attend the rest of the trial session this morning."

Mason walked over to where Lieutenant Tragg was chatting with one of the reporters. "May I see you for a moment, Lieutenant?" he asked.

"Surely," Tragg said, and walked over to a corner of the courtroom.

Mason said, "You testified rather glibly that that pipe was the same this morning."

"Oh, come, Perry," Lieutenant Tragg said, "what's the use of being technical about a deal of that sort. You know and I know it's the same pipe. Of course I didn't sit up all night with it so I could swear it was the same, and I didn't put my initials on it, but I can identify it and I did identify it."

"You made a mistake," Mason said.

Tragg's eyes narrowed. "What do you mean by that?"

Mason said, "I took out the section of pipe, using a chamois skin to pad the jaws of the wrench, and substituted this one which has purely synthetic tool marks in it which were carefully put in there with a pipe wrench where one of the ridges on the jaws had been purposely damaged."

Tragg's face flushed. "Do you realize what you are saying?" he asked.

"I think so."

"You have destroyed evidence in a murder case."

"Oh, no, I haven't," Mason said. "Here, here's the piece of pipe that I took out. That's the genuine pipe. If you think it has any evidentiary value, here it is. I just took the precaution of keeping it in custody."

Tragg's eyes showed his anger.

"But," Mason went on, "the reason I did what I did was that I wanted whoever had actually loosened that gas pipe to feel that his wrench had left distinctive marks on the pipe. For your information, at the morning recess Borden Finchley went to his car drove out to a vacant lot and tossed a wrench into the weeds, then returned to court.

"Now, if I call Borden Finchley as a witness and suddenly spring this on him, I can trap him into some damaging admissions. But *that's* going to make the homicide squad look rather inept.

"If, however, *you* go to work on him during the noon recess, don't let him know there is anything phoney about the markings on that gas pipe, you just might have a confession by two o'clock this afternoon. You're rather skillful at those things, you know.

"And in that event," Mason went on, "no one would ever need to know that there had been any substitution of the gas pipe. The police could have all the credit of solving the case. Hamilton Burger could dismiss the case against the defendant. We could have a happy family reunion and—"

"Where's the vacant lot? Where did he put the wrench?" Tragg asked.

Mason caught Paul Drake's eye, beckoned him over, said, "Paul, get your man who is shadowing Borden Finchley and let him cooperate with Lieutenant Tragg."

The lawyer turned away, smiled at Daphne and said, "See you after lunch, Daphne."

Daphne, her arms tight around Horace Shelby, looked up at him with tear-stained eyes.

Mason moved over to Della Street. "This," he announced, "is one hell of a good time to make our exit."

Chapter TWENTY

When Court reconvened at two o'clock, Hamilton Burger arose to address Judge Kyle.

"If the Court please," he said, "the State has a rather important announcement to make."

"Proceed," Judge Kyle said.

"Thanks to brilliant detective work on the part of the police—in particular the homicide squad and, more particularly, Lieutenant Arthur Tragg," Burger said, "the murder has been solved and the police have a written confession from Borden Finchley.

"I may state briefly that Finchley discovered Ralph Exeter unconscious under such circumstances that he felt he could disconnect the gas feed line, asphyxiate Exeter, and not only escape responsibility for the crime but have the crime blamed upon Horace Shelby.

"In his somewhat warped mind, he felt that if Shelby were executed for the crime, he would be the sole heir. However, his primary purpose was to get rid of the pressure which Ralph Exeter was bringing to bear on him to pay a very substantial gambling debt which had been incurred over a period of some months.

"I therefore wish to make a public acknowledgment of thanks

to Lieutenant Tragg, and the prosecution wishes to dismiss the case against the defendant, Daphne Shelby."

Hamilton Burger sat down.

Judge Kyle, his eyes twinkling, looked at Perry Mason. "Any objections from the defense, Mr. Mason?"

Mason smiled. "None whatever, Your Honor."

Judge Kyle said, "I would be less than fair to myself if I didn't state that this solution constitutes a source of great satisfaction to the Court. The case against the defendant is dismissed and she is released from custody forthwith. Court's adjourned."

A great cheer came from the crowded spectators. Then, as Judge Kyle left the bench, men and women surged forward to congratulate the crying Daphne Shelby, to shake hands with the beaming Horace Shelby.

Lieutenant Tragg sidled over to Perry Mason. "If," he said, "you ever in your life say anything about that substituted gas pipe, I'll throw the book at you."

"Why?" Mason asked innocently. "It was perfectly all right. I took the evidence which you had overlooked into custody for the police. I had it with me, intending to give it to you, but then you produced the perfectly spurious gas pipe which I had used to replace the pipe I had taken, and when you swore that you recognized it as the same pipe, I simply hesitated until I could get you in private to tell you what had happened. And you will remember that I did tell you at the first opportunity."

Tragg said, "You're pretty damned clever, Mason. You got away with it this time, but don't push your luck."

Mason grinned at him and said, "I hate to be static, Lieutenant. I like to push my luck. . . . . Did Finchley tell you how he located Shelby?"

"Las Vegas gamblers located him," Tragg said. "They put the finger on him, and it was agreed Exeter would make one big play for a cash settlement. The Las Vegas man located Shelby for Exeter and then washed his hands of the situation. He didn't want any bad publicity for Las Vegas gambling.

"Finchley wanted a cut. He and his wife were moving Daphne's things, but Finchley went out to the motel to check. He found Exeter asleep—drugged.

"Finchley was all fed up with Exeter and the Las Vegas crowd. He thought he could get Exeter off his neck. He got a wrench from the tool box in his car and unscrewed the gas feed line, drove back and told his wife to cover for him on an alibi."

Mason nodded. "That figures," he said.

Tragg suddenly shot out his right hand, gripped Mason's hand and shook hands cordially.

"Thanks for the buggy ride," he said.

A newspaper photographer exploded a flash bulb and caught the two men shaking hands. A reporter moved over and said to Mason, "What was that Tragg said to you?"

Mason said, "The lieutenant was simply saying that if I had only put my cards on the table with him a little sooner, they would never have arrested Daphne Shelby."

Tragg beamed at the lawyer.

The newspaper reporter seemed puzzled. "Well, why didn't you?" he asked.

Mason turned to where Horace Shelby was writing out a check.

"And cheat myself out of a good fee?" he asked.

The reporter laughed, and the photographer put in a new flash-bulb to hurry over and get a picture of Mason accepting the check.

THE END